Better
Life

Kyle M. Scott

For Raina Gabrielle, whose many worlds I feel blessed to be a part of,
each and every day.

Special thanks to Lindsay Mclean for sticking it out with me while I wrote this number. You're a constant inspiration in my life to do better.

I'd like to give a little shout out to my beta-readers too. Lisa Lee Tone, Jade Velasquez and Mandy Tyra… you guys are invaluable, tough, honest and fair. Now that I've discovered you, I'll most likely be pestering you till the end of time.

Huge thanks, also, to all my readers, both long-term and short-term. Your support is immeasurable. In those dark, endless hours when the journey seems impossible, it's a light that shines bright.

Now let's get to it.

A
Better
Life

Kyle M. Scott

PROLOGUE

With the lightest of touches, the pretty eight-year-old girl brushed her hair aside, revealing a delicate, intelligent face untouched by even the slightest hint of panic or trepidation. She drummed her fingers on her knees carelessly, as though she was merely out for a daytrip with the family and itching to reach their destination.

Was the girl *bored*? Was that it?

Was she bored and day dreaming, like a kid drifting into realms unseen during a particularly lengthy mathematics class? She certainly wasn't *afraid,* Jess thought. At least, she wasn't showing any signs of it. There were no tell-tale tears welling in her luminous green eyes. No dam poised to overspill and unleash a rushing wave of panic and dismay. The panic simply wasn't *there*.

As Jess studied her, the girls wandering eyes met her own from across the van. In them Jess sensed a quietness, a subtle wisdom that seemed to reach far beyond the child's years. The girl sat in silence, looking deep into her eyes, seeming to see beyond the surface level, seeing deeper into Jess that Jess herself felt comfortable with.

Before the child's gaze she felt exposed, naked…guilty.

And, she had to admit, a little nervous.

She wondered what those probing, searching eyes perceived inside of her as they shone, full and round, from behind the parted curtain of jet-black hair. The contrast between the near-mesmeric eyes and the raven hair was both startling and beautiful.

Beautiful or not, though, it did little to help Jess' nerves.

You need to calm down, Jess.

Breathe. Nice and slow. Let your nerves dance the damn jitterbug if they must, but keep your cool, don't let the girl see it. She looks calm, but looks can *be deceiving. She may well be terrified. Poor kid doesn't need you freaking out right alongside her. Feel guilty by all means. You* should *feel guilty. But don't let your mind play tricks on you. Do your part.*

Just do your part.

To her side, the van doors rattled together, a harsh and bracing sound that made her think of chains and captivity and an eight-by-four cell with dried blood on the walls and cockroaches scuttling in the dark corners.

Jess felt like kicking those damn doors open and hurling herself outwards onto the softening tarmac, broken bones be damned.

Instead of making her grand exit from the insane situation she'd gotten herself into, Jess took a deep breath, swallowed her anxiety and flashed the girl a smile she hoped was reassuring. When the girl smiled back, open and warm, Jess' shame only intensified.

In her hands the spare set of keys to the old house clinked together, sounding loud in the van's small confines. She knew that in fumbling with them she was signaling to both her colleague and the girl that she was nervous, but she was helpless to stop it, no matter how the girl or Pete perceived her. The keys jangled noisily as, realizing there was no drawing from the child's all-pervasive calm, she tried to train her mind on something, *anything,* other than the strangely hypnotic eight-year old child.

She finally settled her attention on Pete.

He was sat to the left of the little girl, hunched over so as not to hit his head off the van's roof as it bumped and careened through the desert terrain, careless for the bones of its passengers.

"Are we nearly there?" Jess asked Pete.

Pete's eyes squinted in the gloom, cold and cunning. She knew the man only through the stories her husband had shared but it was obvious that, for whatever reason, he regarded her with intense disdain. The man had small eyes…*rat's eyes,* she mused…yet they seemed somehow smaller still when he set them on her. Two little black holes, poked into an otherwise nondescript face, sucking in light like light was an offence to the man's sensibilities.

Creep.

"He said 'no talking'…so *no* talking," he growled.

'*He*' was Curt, her boyfriend of three years, husband of five years, lover, best friend, and the only person in her life who gave half a damn about her

Currently, he was up-front, steering the rusted, near-derelict van through an unseen landscape. There were no windows back here, only rusting sheet-metal surrounded her, above, to the sides and below her feet. She felt as though she were housed inside a tin can. A sardine, fit for plucking by monstrous fingers from an aluminum coffin.

Nor could she see Curt. That was even more disconcerting. The metal wall that separated the driver's compartment from the van's rear left her feeling a hundred miles apart from him. It didn't help matters that she was stuck back there in the gloomy, uncomfortable tin-can with only Pete's impatient glare and the strange little girl's aura of unearthly calm to keep her company.

Get it together, she scolded herself. *Pete may look like the world's creepiest asshole but Emily sure as hell doesn't...she's just a little girl.*

All she knew of Pete was that he worked alongside Curt at the 'Screw'n'Fix' garage back home in Cider Creek and that he had a real knack for trouble. The relationship between her husband and this angry, gruff individual was, to the best of her knowledge, little more than a 'working' one. Curt hired the man and Pete did as he was told. He'd never once been to Jess and Curt's trailer in the years he'd been in her husband's employ. Not even to drop off parts for work.

He'd been nothing more to Jess than a name without a face, a story without an anchor.

And for these small graces, Lord, I thank thee...

Yet here he was now...barking passed-down orders from her own husband and looking at her like she was something filthy he'd stepped in with his best boots.

Jess could feel his cruel eyes crawl across her flesh.

She couldn't *wait* to have a word with Curt regarding the company he'd brought along on this thing they were doing.

From her front, a quiet, lilting voice: "I'm hungry," the girl said, finally registering Jess, Pete and the situation.

Though startled by the child's sudden words, Jess smiled reassuringly. "We're almost there, sweetheart."

Pete leaned forward. Jess could smell liquor on his breath, sour and stale. "No talking."

Jess ignored him. "We'll be where we're going in just a few more minutes, honey. Then we'll get you something nice to eat, okay?"

The girl didn't return the smile, only nodded and in her strangely calm manner answered, "Okay...thank you." With that, the little girl with the raven hair and the luminous emerald eyes eased back into her 'off-world' serenity.

Jess smiled. "You're welcome."

3

She was a strange child, one entwined in circumstances that were stranger still, but a sweet child at that. Well-mannered, too. Spaced-out or not, Jess liked her.

Just how she'd have liked her own child to be…

Hell no, Jess. Not today. Not on this ride. You can wallow in self-pity when you're on your own clock, but not while you're on the kid's.

Pete hocked loudly and spat on the van floor.

"Lovely," he growled. "Nice to see you two bonding."

Jess, disgusted, went on fingering the spare keys. The girl, content with Jess' answer, had already drifted off on a sea of her own musings. She hadn't lied to the little girl…they *would* be there soon, though the minutes stretched out like hours.

Curt had said the abandoned house was only fifty or so miles from Las Vegas. Sixty, tops.

Las Vegas…

Den of iniquity, rich and fertile pasture for grazing sinners, home of corruptions both subtle and extreme; a world of bright, garish lights, dark festering corners, towering casinos and broken dreams. And the place where they'd snatched up the eight-year old girl who now sat so close to her that Jess swore she could hear her little belly grumbling over the van's engine.

They had to have driven at *least* forty miles out by now. They'd been driving off-road for a huge part of the journey and that would slow things down a touch, but a mile was a mile was a mile and from the way the van was jostling Jess around like a ragdoll on the small wooden bench secured to its side, she figured they weren't moving slowly.

Soon, they'd arrive.

And then what?

Well, then she'd do her part in all this.

She would clean and bathe the girl if needed. She'd feed her. She'd keep her calm, (not that *that* was required, it seemed), and keep her company.

Jess' job in this thing was to make sure the whole plan ran as smoothly as possible. That meant making the girl feel safe, secure, comfortable. The hardest part, Jess surmised, was already over.

They'd managed to abduct the child with no real problems at all. The girl's parents, for all their wealth, power and influence, were apparently just as careless in their protection of their little one as the worst folks back home at Cider-Creek Trailer Park. All that money, all that entitlement, and they'd hired the girl a nanny who barely raised a hand in protest as they snatched the child up.

Perhaps the nanny saw it as poetic justice. A way to get back at the rich and pampered elites who paid her a meagre wage.

That seemed unlikely, though. More likely that they'd held back on their money and simply hired the cheapest carer available. You get what you pay for and you didn't get rich by spending, as Curt was one to say.

Money did not bring class. Not one bit.

But that was no great reveal to Jess. Being the daughter of a tycoon who owned one of the strip's most luxurious high-end casinos afforded her a keen insight into the sorrow that abundance could wrought. She thought of her father's greatest pride now...a bright, shining garish den of hedonism and temptation, a dark beacon in the city of sin, drawing the tourists and gamblers like eager flies to its burning, devouring light.

Skin-deep, he'd seemed a man of immeasurable success, but that skin bled corruption. Privilege, she understood, was oftentimes the road to spiritual impoverishment.

And look where *she'd* ended up, raised by such a high-flying bird...living hand-to-mouth in a two-bit trailer perched on the edge of nowhere, with no future before her and only a dark and sickening past behind.

No...money didn't bring nobility or honor.

Nor did it assure good parenting.

And so here they were; Curt, Pete, herself...

And the girl.

Little Emily.

The daughter of a senator with more corporate interests than political ethics. Heir to great wealth the likes of which most folks could only ever dream of.

Yet with no protection for his kid, a small voice said in her head. *None, at all, unless you counted the barely conscious nanny.*

Jess studied the girl, winking when the girl caught her watching.

The girl smiled, coy and demure.

"Not long now..." Jess worded, quietly mocking Pete and, she hoped, lightening the atmosphere for the faultless girl caught in the black vortex of his mood.

Yes. They'd be there soon.

The old house couldn't be far now.

Jess wondered what it would look like.

According to Curt, it had stood out there in the barren desert, uninhabited, for years. Perhaps for as long as three or four decades. Perhaps even longer.

Empty.

Forgotten.

Abandoned, until she and her companions had come along, with their plans and their dreams of escaping the dead-end lives they all lived in.

Jess allowed herself to reach over and take the little girl's hand in her own. She squeezed reassuringly.

Emily squeezed back.

Pete shook his head in disgust. It seemed the whole spectrum of his repertoire was spit, curse, growl and scowl. Not necessarily in that order.

Both she and Emily ignored him.

Jess studied those luminous, hypnotic emerald eyes, marveling at the little girl's beauty. How perfect her skin looked, unblemished by time, unravaged by woes. How bright her gaze, brimming with innocence and untapped potential, keen to be unchained and set free.

Yet as she gazed into the girl's ethereal eyes...

Jess saw something.

Or thought she had.

She was smiling at the girl as their eyes met, yet in the dark reflection of the child's pupils Jess could *swear* that...just for a second...she'd seen herself screaming.

Screaming, lost and alone, in the darkness.

The vision passed as quickly as it had surfaced.

The van sped on through the gathering Mojave dusk, while the desert held its breath.

PART ONE

Hopes and Dreams

1

"We're here!" Curt shouted from the front.

His voice was muffled by the thick sheet of metal that separated the cabin from the driver's compartment, but to Jess it rang like a Sunday church bell on a summer's morning. Her legs were beginning to cramp, and she desperately needed to pee. Besides all that, Pete was still doing his thing; looking and acting like a hardened thug with all the scruples of a wild dog. She'd be glad to be away from him and inside the house at last.

"You ready?" she asked Emily.

The girl nodded.

"Can we just fucking *go*, already?" Pete huffed.

Jess reached for the handle, pulled down hard and swung the van's rear-door wide.

Fresh air washed over her and she breathed deep. Shuffling to the exit, she climbed from the van, glad to feel the sand and dirt beneath her feet. She reached in and took Emily gently by the hand. The girl squinted as she stepped into the soft warmth of the evening. Dark had yet to settle on the land and the fiery-red skies, that seemed to reach on forever, were a far cry from the dusty, shadowed confines of their ride.

Hopping lightly from the van's interior, Emily's lightness of touch immediately intensified. She gripped Jess' hand, held on tight as they turned together and took in the house; a first look for them both.

It looked like something from a fairy tale.

Or perhaps from an old movie; the type Jess' mother used to love watching. Something alight and shimmering in glorious Technicolor, starring Clark Gable, or maybe Cary Grant.

She quickly cast aside thoughts of her mother, wary as always of where they'd lead, and studied the huge two-story house in all its pre-industrial splendor.

It looked a lot older than Curt had surmised.

The white paint, once surely dazzling in the dusk's waning light, was faded, giving the place a more ancient look than it would otherwise have. Some parts of the roof looked close to collapsing in on themselves, bent beneath the will of a hundred seasons. The awning that surrounded the borders of the roof hung loose in places. Instead of water, weeds spilled over the sides of the gutters up there, swaying in the evening breeze. The house's windows were almost all surprisingly intact. Of the nine she counted, only one on the upper floor was completely shattered, while two to its left were badly cracked. Curtains, so worn they looked like bound wraiths watching the world beyond their borders, clung to the glass, hungry for light. Lights shone in two of the downstairs windows, though Jess could see little of the house's interior.

The light looked artificial. No flickering of flame. Had Lisa brought a generator with her in place of candles?

Two old Juniper trees swayed languidly in the gentle desert breeze to either side of the house, affording it a pleasing symmetry as they lent in protectively over the roofing. The front porch housed a rocking chair for two, sat to the side of an old oak door that stood wide open.

And behind and around this wonderful old representation of a time when men were men and women wore corsets - the shimmering stars shone from the heavens above, piercing the slowly darkening, purple-red skies with their ancient light.

"It's beautiful," the small child said in a soft, quiet voice.

"It sure is," Jess agreed. "I feel like Scarlett in *Gone with the Wind.*"

"*Gone with the wind*? What's that?"

"It's the name of an old movie. A very *good* one. I'll tell you all about it later, if you like."

"I love old movies. I watch them all the time in my room…the black and white ones. I'd like that."

"I would too, Emily," she said, smiling down at the girl.

The conversation was cut short when, from the left side of the van, Curt appeared.

"Damn!" Curt bemoaned. "That was a bumpy freaking ride! Made Jell-O of my butt! You guys okay?"

Pete nodded and said nothing.

Jess, still holding the captive girl's hand, said, "We're fine. Good to be out of that thing, though. You think it was tough in the front, try being in the *back.*"

Curt laughed. She felt a swell of love for the man. He may have been a lowly mechanic in a run-down garage amidst the dust and death of the desert, but he was a good man, a kind man.

9

Not like her father.

Not like him.

Curt moved towards her, grinning, and placed a palm on her cheek. Speaking quietly, he said, "You sure you're okay? I know *he* can be a bit of a handful…"

As if on cue, Pete growled. "Okay, now that we've all sucked each other's dicks, can we get inside? I need a fucking drink."

"Hey!" Curt snapped. "Not in front of the kid, you understand me!?"

Pete spit in the sand. "Whatever…" He skulked off, taking in the house.

"Yeah…*whatever*…"

Curt looked down at the little girl, his face softening. "And you, sweetheart…how are you?"

"I'm okay, I guess," Emily answered, dutifully.

Curt smiled. "Good. That's good. You know that nothing's going to happen to you, right? We're not going to hurt you, honey. No one is. This'll all be over soon, I promise. I want you to know that you're safe here."

Emily nodded. "Okay."

"And in the meantime, you have my girl here…" He pointed at Jess. "…to keep you company. The house is pretty darn cool too, and my *other* friend is inside and has brought along all sorts of toys and things for you. You'll be fine. Try to think of this as a holiday with friends."

Again, a small nod. "Okay."

"Okay…Oh, and ignore *him.*" He nodded at Pete. "He's a bit of a grump when he doesn't get his sleep, but you won't see much of him anyway, darlin'" Curt ruffled the girl's hair and gave Jess a soft peck on the cheek. "We'd better get inside."

From the small patch of dried-up lawn that separated the grand old home from the scorched desert, Pete shouted over his shoulder. "Can we get a fucking move on!? We don't need to parade the kid out here for all the world to see, do we?"

"I hear *one more curse word* in front of that little girl, I'm going to cut off a piece of you that's too small to sew back on, Pete!" hollered a woman's voice.

Jess grinned when she heard the familiar and amusingly fearsome voice pour from the old house's doorway.

Curt strolled up the lawn to the porch steps, embracing the portly woman stood there as Pete entered the old house, his face burning red.

"Hi, sis," Curt said, kissing the big woman on a flushed, rounded cheek.

Emily, Jess thought to herself, still grinning, *meet Lisa.*

2

"Not bad...not bad at all," said Jess, admiring the bedroom as she entered.

It wasn't false positivity. The room was nice.

In fact, it was a whole lot nicer than the flea-bitten, two-room sardine-can that she and Curt called home. She wondered briefly what had made the owners leave this place. It was glorious, even when compared to her own bedroom when she was a child, living in the lap of luxury, spoiled for material want by parents bereft of anything else worthwhile to offer.

She thought of her old bedroom, full of fineries, overlooking the lights of Vegas from a dizzying height atop her father's grandest hotel, and thought, *I'd take this here room over that one, any day of the working week.*

Jess watched as the young girl's eyes flitted from toy to toy, book to book. There were dolls and plushies of all shapes and sizes; bears, Disney characters, a large Scooby-Doo replete with goofy smile and lolling tongue, a collection of small, brightly colored ponies that Jess couldn't place from any cartoon she knew. The books ranged from young adult paperbacks to coloring-books complete with handy selections of crayons or pencils affixed to the covers. There was an old, Victorian dollhouse, inhabited by small forest critters; mice, foxes, badgers. The room itself was dimly lit by a small bedside lamp decorated with stars and crescent moons. The bed, though old and worn, looked soft. Clean and comfortable sheets - supplied by the always reliable Lisa, of course - were the icing on the cake.

Emily would be fine here.

Jess watched with pleasure as the young girl sprung onto the bed, light as air, and immediately made for one of the young-adult fiction novels.

Quietude in a person was not definitive proof of their intellect, but during the ride out to the house, Jess had suspected the girl to be not *only* self-assured, but admirably bright for her age. She hadn't been wrong.

"I've heard of this one!" Emily declared, holding aloft a book which featured some sort of looking glass on the cover. Jess couldn't make out the title as Emily tossed it aside and picked up another. Then another. "And this. And this!"

Jess laughed. "And what about the toys? You still play with toys, right?"

Emily stopped fiddling with the books and drew Jess a look that said, '*are you kidding me*?'.

"I'm *eight*, Jess. I *love* toys."

Jess tried to conceal her amusement. "That's great to hear. We wouldn't want all these cool toys to go to waste, would we?"

"Nope!"

Jess laughed aloud. Damn. The girl was cute.

Suddenly the giddy excitement seemed to ebb from the girl and she flopped back on the bed, her head landing on one of the pillows propped against the headboard.

"Jess?" she asked.

"Yes, honey?"

"How long are you going to keep me here?"

Jess felt her face flush red. "It shouldn't be long, sweetheart. No longer than we need to, I promise."

"You're wanting money from my daddy, aren't you?"

Jess sat down gently on the side of the bed. The bed sunk in such a manner that her thigh brushed against the girl's. She felt the warmth of the child and appreciated the contact.

"Something like that. We're not bad people, honey. I want you to know that. What the man said outside was the truth. We won't hurt you. We just need a little something to help us live our lives better, that's all."

"Are you poor?" Emily asked, bluntly.

Jess laughed. "Yes, I suppose we *are* poor."

"How come?"

"That's just how the world works, honey. Not everyone has the chance to reach their potential, even when they deserve it."

"What about your mummy and daddy? Can't you ask them?"

"My mum is dead, honey."

"And your daddy?"

Jess saw her father leaning over her, drool running from his lips and falling onto her face as she trembled beneath his weight. His shadow taking up the whole world. His breath sour, his nose peppered with a

13

white dust that seemed to drive him to madness. His groin pressed against her leg. A hardness there…

Jess smiled to conceal her sadness. "He's dead, too, Emily."

Emily rested her open hand on Jess' leg. "I think you're nice, Jess. I think *you'll* reach *your* potential," she said, with a reassurance beyond her years.

The assurance with which Emily spoke was almost enough to convince Jess of it. Almost. "I hope so, kiddo. I hope so."

"I promise I'll be good. I'll do everything you need me to do. But one thing…"

"Yeah, what's that?"

"Can I have something to eat? I'm starved."

Jess laughed, stood up and made for the bedroom door. "Course you can, Emily. I'll be up in five minutes with the best darn sandwich this side of the Mojave. That woman down there…my friend…she *really knows* her way around a sandwich. Prepare to be dazzled!"

Emily giggled.

Seeing the girl smile, she wondered why she'd felt so uneased by her demeanor back in the van. "When I come back and…only if you like…you and I can play together for a while. Maybe read a book or do some painting. Whatever you want to do."

"I'd like to do *any* of those."

"Me too." Jess opened the bedroom door. She passed through and made to close it behind her. It pained her to say what she had to say next. She felt sick to her stomach as she uttered the words. "I need to lock this door, Emily…"

"I know. It's fine."

"I'm so sorry."

"Really… it's okay," the girl answered, un-phased. "I have my books!"

Jess smiled then shut the door. She bolted the latch, hating herself for it, took a deep breath and made for the rickety wooden staircase that led to the ground floor of the house where her companions awaited her arrival.

She was halfway down before she paused, confused.

She thought back over the conversation with the girl, replaying it in her mind, trying to remember every word they'd shared as best she could.

Something didn't sit right.

What was it, though?

The girl had been much more communicative since arriving at the house, but that wasn't it. She'd seemed delighted with the room, too.

So, what's eating at you?

She played the conversation over again, saw the girl wearing that wry expression when she asked her if she liked toys.

'I'm eight, Jess...'

That was it!

'Jess...'

How in the hell *does she know my name?*

3

Curt was sat at the end of the table. He stared down at the sandwich Lisa had made for him. It looked delicious; fresh tomatoes, sliced and placed over smoked ham, garnished with a condiment of her own devising, (one which she'd never share with another living soul, even on pain of death), and crisp lettuce, all squeezed between two thick slices of whole-wheat bread.

The condiment was the special ingredient that sealed the deal. It was out of this world.

Yet Curt had no appetite.

Lisa was over by the kitchen sink, staring out into the fading light. Pete, Curt's workmate and a grade-a asshole at the very best of times, was working his way to the bottom of a bottle of Becks. Not the first bottle he'd had, either.

And was that the smell of liquor I detected on his breath earlier?

Yeah…yeah, I'm pretty sure it was.

Let it go. For now.

If he keeps at it…

He won't.

But if he does…

He heard Jess coming down the stairs before he saw her and immediately looked up, not wanting to miss a thing.

Holy Jesus, she was something.

Her shoulder-length hair - a dark and shining brown – swayed from side to side as she skipped down the remaining stairs. Her full breasts pressed against the *Velvet Underground* t-shirt she wore, disfiguring a smirking, oh-so-cool looking *Lou Reed* as he oozed drug-chic. Tight jeans clung to her long, lithe legs, tightening further at the ankles. She wore sandals that showed off her slender feet. Her toenails were painted grass-green.

It was her eyes, though, that truly took his breath away.

Behind those beautiful almond eyes of hers resided her true beauty. Past the pain, past the sadness…a determination and will to fight that had quickly won his heart. Her soul.

And after all these years together, not for a single moment had he felt anything for Jess besides love, admiration and an ever-replenishing bucketful of good old-fashioned lust.

She was one hell of a woman.

And she was a survivor.

Just like he was.

It pained Curt that he'd been forced to make Pete ride back there with her and the kid, but Pete was a wild driver and Curt had no intentions of putting either the kid *or* Jess in harm's way, *especially* when the moron was already getting his buzz on from the booze.

Curt sincerely hoped that, for Jess, being able to ride along with the little girl made up for Pete's unsavory company. Jess' heart was as vibrant as her smile and she positively *loved* children. They had no kids of their own, he and Jess, not with each other and not with anyone else, and he knew the hurt it caused his wife. Spending time with the girl would be good for Jess.

I just wish it were under different circumstances.

Can't always get what you want in this life.

It had been a good idea, having her ride with the kid, despite Jess' fragile condition, both physically and emotionally.

It was worth the risk, he told himself, *just to see her glowing as she'd climbed into the van with the kid.*

Curt watched the woman he loved descend the stairs and move towards him. She wore a bemused expression on her face, as though something troubled her. Perhaps not '*troubled*', but, certainly, something was on her mind.

There was no time to inquire before Jess spoke.

"Emily's hungry," she said.

"Aren't we all," Pete interjected.

Lisa huffed from her place by the window, "Then eat something, Pete, instead of hitting the fucking bottle like it's prohibition-era Chicago. What are you, an idiot?"

Curt stifled a laugh. Jess' silence spoke volumes.

His sister, Lisa, was a feisty creature and not one to be messed with. She always managed to shut Pete up real fast. That tough-guy exterior of his never failed to crumble and dissolve when Curt's older sibling was around.

As Jess pulled out a chair and sat by his side at the table, Curt watched Pete with amusement, curious to see how the man would react.

"I was just *saying*," Pete grumbled.

He sounded like a ten-year-old kid, freshly scolded.

Lisa ignored him. Over her shoulder she asked, "I have some sandwiches here, Jess. You wanna grab a selection and take them up to the little princess? She could use something to eat, poor child. Stuck in that van for so long with nothing to fill her belly."

"She was just saying the same thing," Jess responded. "They all made with your secret sauce, Mama?"

"You damn well know it, sister."

"Nice! She'll love 'em."

"And don't you mind Pete. He means no harm. Just a miserable son of a bitch, is all. I should know...I *married* him, once upon a time."

Jess blurted out laughter, Curt damn near choked.

"Give it a rest, Lisa," Pete moaned. "I ain't in the mood for your shit."

Lisa, Curt realized, was far from finished. "I saw the way you were talking in front of that precious little girl, Pete. You're a no-good sonofabitch and ain't no one will ever convince me of anything different. Just what in the hell are you doing here, anyway?"

Pete slammed his near-empty bottle of Becks on the table. "It was my goddamn *idea*, woman!"

Lisa noticeably flinched when Pete's bottle hit the table. Not for the first time, he wondered if, behind the bravado, she feared Pete. And if so, why?

If I ever find out that he hurt her...

Lisa went back to staring out the window. As an afterthought, she added. "That was it," Lisa responded, sounding far less playful. "But hell, don't feel too good about it. Even a broken clock tells the right time, twice daily. You managed only once in over a decade."

Jess grimaced, sensing the atmosphere stretch from gentle ribbing to something more serious.

"The only damn thing I ever done right was leaving your fat ass in the dust."

"Hey!" Curt snarled. "You don't *ever* talk to my sister that way again, you hear me? You do and you'll be scooping up your teeth with a spoon,

18

Pete! Where I come from, we treat women with respect. Mind your manners!"

Pete piped down quick, though he continued to sulk.

What Lisa said had been true, Pete was a mean, miserable bastard, but he was weak. He saw himself as a lion, but lions were courageous, noble creatures.

Pete was many things, but nobility and courage were not among his attributes.

What he *was,* was an ex-con. The type of asshole who coasted by on the misfortune of others. The kind who rarely earned and often took. The only reason he'd even *accepted* the job at Curt's garage had been down to it being a prerequisite of his parole. The only reason Curt had *offered* it, was down to his older sister being married to the man at the time.

What Lisa had once seen in Pete, Curt had no idea, yet while it was true that Pete was a no-good drunk and a leech, the depth of Lisa's hatred for the man had often seemed…severe…to Curt. Again, he wondered, as he often did, if there was more to their break-up than Pete simply being Pete.

In the end, it made little difference; Lisa and Pete had a kid together – a handsome, gentle boy of ten-years-old, named Billy – and so were tied together for the duration of this weird old thing called life. And family was family.

Worried for little Billy, Curt had offered the father of his nephew the job and had held his tongue and curbed his patience ever since, even during the divorce and in the years afterwards.

The parents being divorced didn't mean his nephew shouldn't be provided for, so he'd kept Pete on as a mechanic - the one and only skill the man had at his disposal.

And until this whole…road trip…had begun, Curt had also managed to keep Pete away from his *own* home life *and* away from Jess. It ate away at him that she was even *near* the unscrupulous bastard…as though his sly, insidious nature were an affront to Jess' purity. As though it could taint her, somehow.

But needs must.

And the whole crazy, desperate thing they were doing *had* been Pete's idea.

Jess let out a rasping cough, pulling Curt from thoughts of his workmate. She reached into her shirt pocket to retrieve a hanky and raised it to her lips. "Excuse me," she said quietly. She looked frail, worn-out, weak. Curt thought he saw a trace of crimson on the handkerchief and felt something twist and churn inside him.

"Are you okay, baby?" he asked her, worriedly.

"I'm fine. Really."

"You sure?"

"I'm sure."

"Listen, if you need to lie down…"

"Curt…baby…I'm fine. Just lost my breath for a moment there. Steep stairs, you know…?"

He nodded.

He knew, alright.

Then Lisa was by their side, holding out a glass of water to Jess. She accepted it gratefully and drank the full glass down in one go. "Better," she gasped. "Thank you, Lisa."

"Anytime, darlin'."

"So," Pete asked, reaching for another beer. "We going to do this fucking thing, or what?"

4

Jess kissed Curt as he stepped from the porch and onto the lawn, making once more for the van, with Pete in tow.

Together, the two men silently entered the old run-down vehicle, slammed their doors shut and got the engine running. It sounded deafeningly loud amidst the uncanny silence of the desert, where only the droning mantra of nestling Mormon crickets cut through the eerie silence. There was a second when Jess was sure the van's engine wouldn't turn over. She watched intently, waiting for the cliché, but it never came.

It wouldn't have mattered a great deal anyway; Lisa had arrived much earlier in the day to set things up for little Emily and had her Jeep parked out back and out of sight. There was little chance they'd find themselves stranded out there in the Mojave wilds, regardless of the van's less-than-confidence inspiring condition.

She watched it pull away, kicking up plumes of dirt in its wake as it disappeared into the gathering dusk.

She was startled when Lisa appeared at her side, as if from nowhere. "Jesus, Lisa! You half scared me to death!"

"Sorry, darlin'. Is that those two off to make a buck?"

"Yeah..." Her own voice sounded distant in her ears.

Lisa rested a heavy hand on Jess' shoulder, squeezing. "Don't you worry about Curt, Jess. He's got a good head on his shoulders, that one. And he loves you mightily. There's no fire that man wouldn't walk through, just to set you straight and see you right. Just keep that in mind and trust in his judgement."

"I do."

"You should. That man has a love for you that most of us gals only ever dream of finding. Before you came along..." Lisa paused.

"What?"

"Before you came along, I worried for him. I mean *really* worried for him. You know how we lost our mother, right?"

"He's told me all of it. The breakdown, the depression..."

"It hit him hard when she began to go downhill. I'm guessing he didn't up and tell you the part I played in all of it?"

Jess frowned. "No."

Lisa sighed. "That's because I *didn't* play a part in it, Jess. I was drinking myself to death, lost in the bottle, when our mother took ill. I wasn't there for her. I wasn't there for *him*."

"I'm sure you did your best."

"I'd like to think so. I'd like to tell myself that I did, but that's horseshit. I should have been there for them both. My mother died without her daughter by her side. And Curt, he needed his sister. He needed me and I was swimming at the bottom of a glass of gin. There was no one else to help him handle her death. And it was a *slow* death, Jess. Slow and painful. Curt watched our momma rot away to nothing before the good lord took her. He was too young to carry that burden alone, but when he needed me the most…"

"Curt loves you, Lisa. He really does."

"I know he does…I know it, but I also know I don't deserve it." Lisa stared off towards the road. Far off in the distance, a thin plume of dust kicked up…the men, gradually vanishing from sight.

Jess felt cold as she followed Lisa's eyes down the long road. "We all make mistakes," she said.

"Not like mine, we don't. Curt acts strong. He does his best, but he was always a fragile boy and it only got worse after nine months of sitting by our mother's bedside while she wasted away. It broke him, Jess. It broke my brother and that's on me."

The van having finally faded from sight, Lisa turned to Jess. "I'm getting off track. What I mean to say is that he was lost until the day he found you. You brought him hope, honey. All the therapy in the world couldn't have put Curt back together again after he laid our mom in her grave. But you could. And you did. You're his life, Jess. His whole life. And *that*…" she said, injecting a forced lightness into her voice, "is why you needn't worry your pretty head about Curt. You know how smart he is, not to mention how focused he is on this thing we're doing, because he's doing it for you. I promise, this'll all be fine."

"And what about Pete?"

"Huh?"

"Can we rely on Pete?"

Lisa huffed. "Well, that's a different story, but he looks up to Curt. He'd rather eat shit than admit it, but he does. And Pete's not all bad. He pays his alimony and he sees little Billy whenever he can. He's had a shitty life and its hardened his heart, but he means well. It was Pete who approached Curt with this whole idea, don't forget. Without Pete, none of this would be happening. He did a good thing, Jess."

"He wasn't doing it for Curt or for me, though, was he? Pete is in this for himself."

"The man simply saw an opportunity and he took it, darlin'. Pete needs the money, too. Maybe not as much as you guys need it...going through what you're going through and all...but, between you and me, he's in real deep with some real mean bastards back in Vegas and this is his ticket out of a six-by-four hole in the desert. Fear is a powerful catalyst for action, little sister. It'll keep him on the straight and narrow while he needs to be."

Jess thought of the beers she'd watched him chug down, the smell of liquor on his breath. "I hope so."

"Trust me...there's nothing that scares that man more than those hoodlums back in the city. He fucks *this* up, he's in serious trouble and he knows it. The only thing that jackass fears more than that Pete-size hole in the desert, is spiders."

Taken aback, Jess laughed. It felt fine to release the tension. *"Spiders?"*

"Yup. Big ones, little ones...doesn't matter. If it has eight legs and crawls on a wall, he's terrified of it. Hell, back when we were living together, if he saw one of those devils in the house, he'd be out the door and in the yard, dancing the jitterbug and yelling like a frightened kid for me to kill the damn thing and save his ass."

Jess giggled, thinking of Pete's hard exterior, brought to heel by a harmless spider.

"And you know what else...? After I'd gone and killed whichever little thing had put the shits on him, he'd spend the rest of the day or night hunting for more. He'd sit there on our couch and scan the walls like a soldier in a trench scanning for the Viet-cong. Never saw anything like it in my life! Damned near drove me crazy, watching his head darting around like a startled bird's. I never knew – men being what they are – that they could concentrate that long on one thing, besides what's between a lady's legs, a'course. But he'd stare at those walls for hours, Jess. *Hours...*"

Both women were laughing now, the tension subsiding. Jess felt a powerful surge of love for her sister-in-law. The big woman, for all her sharp edges, sure had a way about her.

When the mutual laughter finally subsided, Lisa sighed. "So...as you can assuredly now see, when it comes to protecting his own ass, Pete can be one *driven* son of a bitch. Try not to worry too much."

Jess looked out across the vast expanse of sand and grit, imagining Curt out there with that sleaze, alone with him. Lisa had muted her apprehension some, but a coward and a gambling man was one to be watched and an animal cornered, the most dangerous kind.

With her stomach tight, and her nerves taut, she voiced her real fear. "I feel like he uses Curt to fix all his own problems, Lisa. Like he's exploited Curt's nature and heart to get what he needs, you know?"

"And he *has*, Jess...he *has*. There ain't no denying it. But that's how the world works, sometimes. There are those exploiting and those *being* exploited. Most of the time, those being exploited don't see hide nor hair of a happy ending, but you and Curt...you *both* get to come out of this on top. He uses you and you use him. Everyone's happy."

"And what about *you*, Lisa?"

Lisa laughed. "Me? Curt's my brother, darlin'. There's nothing I wouldn't do to see him happy. And..." She squeezed Jess tighter still. "I've grown kind of fond of having you around, too."

Jess leaned her head back, resting it on the buxom woman's ample bosom as she watched the sun sink over the mountains, feeling much like a child herself. "Thanks, Mama."

Lisa stroked Jess' soft brown hair with a tenderness Jess' own mother had never expressed. "You're welcome. But don't you be calling me 'Mama'. I may look like roadkill, but I'm younger than you might think. Any more of that 'n' I'll have you up and into your bed without no supper!"

"Which reminds me..."

"Gotta feed the little one," Lisa finished for her. "How is she?"

Jess thought for a moment before answering. "She's fine, I think. She doesn't seem phased at all by any of this. She knows what's going on, or at least I think she does, but she's taking it all in her stride. It's a little disconcerting to be honest."

"Well, it shouldn't be. She's relaxed because she has you here, honey. We both knew this whole thing wouldn't work unless you were here to keep the girl mellow. You got a comforting way with you, sweetheart. It makes my heart break, when I think of you and Curt, not having a little one of your own and all."

"Thank you," Jess replied, cutting the big woman off, wary to hear it, to dredge up old hurt.

Lisa changed the conversation. "Well…what I mean to say is, that little girl will be fine. She'll get through all this, because she'll have you to lead her through it."

Jess watched the last rays of the sun fall over the desert horizon, washing the mountains in a near-black shadow that made them look almost unreal; a hallucinogenic vision without the psychedelics. She let her gaze lift from the fiery halo that ringed the world and up into the purple, cloudless skies above her head. There was a chill in the air that seemed to seep through her skin and cling to her bones; the Mojave whispering sweet nothings to the day, as it bid it goodnight.

"This is wrong, though. You know that, right, Lisa?"

"Snatching an innocent little girl off the street from the arms of her nanny and scurrying off with the poor kid to hold her ransom? Now how could *that* ever be wrong?"

Jess laughed, but it rang hollow. "If we get caught…"

"We *won't* get caught. You saw what happened. Pete may be a pussycat, but he looks damn near lethal and he can play 'mean' better than most. Most likely because he *would* be the meanest bastard in the state of Nevada, if he wasn't such a giant pussy. After a dose of *his* grisly face, that nanny will be straight back home and relaying his orders just as precise as you like. You can believe there'll be no cops involved. It'll be a simple trade-off. The senator's daughter for the three million. Done and dusted.

"What if he *does go* to the cops?"

"Her daddy?"

"Yeah."

"He won't."

"But what *if*…?"

"You really see that happening, Jess?"

25

"Maybe…I mean, it's possible. He'll be scared, Lisa. He might act irrationally."

"It won't happen, darlin'."

"How can you be so sure, though?"

"Jess…that girl's father is as corrupt as the day is long. How in the hell do you think a snake like Pete ever learned what he learned about the man? All politicians are sons of bitches, flashing their dicks around the internet, stealing from the working classes, cuddling up to lobbyists 'n' those fucks on television that call themselves journalists. They're all sociopaths, but that guy, he takes the cake. He'll not want the law involved in all this. He probably has more skeletons in his closet than he has over-expensive suits. He'll do as he's asked and he'll say no more on the matter. Really. You and Curt will be over the state line and making for Mexico before anyone knows a darn thing. And me, I can go back to my boy and my life, knowing I did a good thing for two people I love very much…"

"And for one asshole."

Lisa nodded stoically. "*And* for one asshole."

Jess chuckled. "Look on the bright side….at least your Billy will still have his dad around him and not murdered and buried out there somewhere by gangsters." She waved her hand towards the endless desert.

"You say that like it's a good thing." Lisa rued. "Come on back inside. Let's get that beautiful little girl fed and watered. It's going to be a long night for the poor thing."

"You really think they'll be okay?"

"Course they will! The payphone is only fifty or so miles out east. They'll be back before you know it. Just a few hours at the very most. Now come on, I'm freezing my boobs off out here and they're about the only bait I got left when I go fishing for a strong hard man to keep me warm!"

"Lisa!"

"Come on, Miss Scawllet," the big woman drawled, feigning the familiar southern cadence of the famous, if somewhat racially provocative, nanny from *Gone with the Wind*. "Lessa git you inside afore y'all's catch ya death'a'cold, now! Laws, yes!"

"You're terrible!"

"'Terrible' is subjective," Lisa said. "Now get moving, before we both get our delicious asses bitten by rattlers!"

5

Curt's eyes followed the old dusty road. He focused all his attention on the sparse illumination the van's headlights cast on the deserted two-lane. With his window rolled down, he let himself enjoy the cool night air wafting in as it blew his hair back, caressing his face, filling his lungs.

In the passenger seat, Pete sat quietly. He rested his tattooed arm on the sill and blew smoke out into the night, chasing each exhalation with a fresh sip of beer.

How many was that he'd sunk back now? Three? Four?

Curt knew the man could handle his drink. Pete couldn't handle much *else* in this life, but he could hold his alcohol. What was the old saying?

The blacksmith's dog...so used to the embers it never gets burnt.

That was Pete. He drank like he lived...carelessly and with no thought for consequences.

He's still functioning. Just let it go for now.

He's an idiot, but he's dangerous. Mean as a rattler. Do you really want to start something with the guy when there's no need?

No need yet...

Cross that bridge when you come to it.

Also, he didn't want to appear ungrateful after Pete had given he and Jess an 'out' from their dire predicament.

You're not about to let things go south, either, despite what he brought to the table. There are limits to gratitude.

I'll have a word, soon, he decided.

Doing his best to remain calm, he followed the road as it crept on and on into the night. He may not have uttered a single word the whole journey, were it not for Pete, who tossed another empty bottle out into the roadside, belched, and said, "So how do you think it'll go down?"

Curt paused to think of the right response. "It'll go down just as we figured, Pete. We get to the payphone and they'll be waiting for our call. What time is it?"

Pete studied his wristwatch. "Coming up on ten-to-nine. Don't worry. We'll be there on time."

"I know."

"Even if we're a little late, something tells me the kid's parents will wait."

"I said I *know*. It's going to be fine. We're…what…five minutes out? That'll give us time to get there, compose ourselves and make the call."

"And you'll do the talking?"

Curt gave Pete a withering look. "Yeah, Pete. I'll do the talking. Charm isn't one of your finer points."

Pete grunted as he stretched low to the van's floor, found an unopened bottle down there and rose back up, satisfied with his haul.

This is getting ridiculous.

Can't he lay off the booze for one goddam night!?

"Do me a favor, Pete…go slow on that, okay? We don't make the drop-off until dawn. It'd be nice if you weren't wasted, or hungover, when the time comes."

Pete saluted. "Last one. Scout's honor."

"So," Curt asked, letting the matter go for now. "What do you think of the girl?"

Pete popped the bottle-top. "Tell you the truth, the little shit creeps me out, man. She was calm as Keanu Reeves back there on the ride up to the house. What kind of fucking kid gets snatched out of an adult's arms, loaded into a van and carted off to who-knows-where without breaking a sweat? Not *one* fucking teardrop, did she shed, Curt. Not *one*."

"Maybe she's in shock," Curt said, worried.

"Yeah, maybe. Or maybe she's a little fucking freak."

Curt tried to keep his voice even. "She's just a little kid, Pete. How about you go easy on the name-calling?"

"Whatever, man. I'm telling you, the kid's not right."

Not right, Curt mused. *You'd know all about that, wouldn't you, buddy?*

Ahead, the road turned a wide left. Not long now till they'd arrive at the payphone. Pete had gone ahead days earlier to make sure the damn thing worked, and it had, but Curt remained on edge.

This whole thing felt so *wrong*.

How had it come to this?

How did a man go from being a simple mechanic to a child-abductor in the space of a few days?

In his mind, Jess' face flashed like distant lightning. He felt a great swelling of love. With it came pain. He knew, as he always had, the answer to this and all questions.

It's for her, Curt. It's always been for her.

And it always will be.

"Okay," Pete said, dragging him from his thoughts. "Slow down. The pay-phone is on the left-hand side, just over there."

Curt hit the brakes, slowing the van to a gradual stop just in front of the old phone. It stood alone, looking alien amidst the endless nothingness of the desert, a construct of man's ingenuity in a terrain where 'man' had no God-given right to build anything. He was glad of it, though. It sure as hell made their job much easier.

Phones like this were scattered throughout the many byways and highways that cut like concrete knives through the desert plains. Periodically maintained by unseen engineers, they were always available for the hapless traveler whom fate favored to strand out in the middle of nowhere.

Shutting off the engine, Curt got out of the van. He stretched his legs. It had been a short drive from the old house, but the van was small and his legs were already cramping. Pete remained inside the vehicle, watching from the side window.

"Gimme the number," Curt demanded.

"No problem, senor." They'd brought no technology with them at all on this venture, fearing the all-seeing eye of the law and its endless powers of observation. In a world where everyone was monitored every moment, technology was an absolute no-go. The family's home number, they'd chosen to keep only on a small piece of paper. Minimal detection, minimal risk. The pay-phone...far enough from where they were holed up, in case something went awry.

"It's in the front." Pete tossed his wallet.

Curt caught it and moved towards the phone, opening the worn leather and searching within as he did so. He found the number quickly, pulled it from the leather folds and stopped by the payphone.

As he reached for the phone a tumbleweed rolled silently out of the darkness beyond the van's headlights, bounced lightly across the road then disappeared into the gathering gloom. Curt watched it continue its silent pilgrimage with a shiver.

Christ almighty, it's eerie out here.

Somewhere out in the endless night a wild dog howled; a hollow and despairing sound, it sliced through the deafening silence and set his teeth on edge.

"Okay Curt", he told himself. "It's now or never."

He picked up the phone from its cradle, held it to his ear and with his other hand he dialed the number on the small piece of paper.

The line connected and on the other side, far from the fevered night and the cold requiem of the desert's song, a phone began to ring.

6

Jess unlocked and opened the bedroom door to find Emily sat atop the old bed, calmly reading one of the many comic books that Lisa had picked up for her.

Eschewed the novels and went for the comics.

Still a kid at heart, despite her smarts.

I like that.

Jess studied the comic's cover, where *Superman* stood proud and tall before the old red white and blue, while the girl's eyes pored over the contents within. Her small hands held the comic in front of her face, only inches from her little button nose, as though she was trying to breathe in its magic.

"Any good?" Jess asked.

"It's awesome," Emily said. "But I like *Batman* better."

Jess smiled. "Don't we all, sweetheart. I brought you some sandwiches. Sorry it took so long. We had stuff to discuss down there. Grown-up stuff."

"It's fine," the girl said, still enrapt in the comic-book's world. "It smells nice…the sandwich…"

"They taste as nice as they smell, trust me. My friend downstairs knows a thing or two about cooking."

"My mom's a good cook, too."

Jess felt guilt gnawing within her.

You took her from her mommy.

You…a stranger.

And what must her mom be feeling now? Alone, lost, helpless, terrified.

This was wrong.

This was all *wrong, Jess, and you know it.*

She frowned and sat on the bed by the girl. "You'll be with her again soon, I promise."

The girl said nothing.

"My other friends have gone to call your mommy and daddy. They're probably talking to them right now," she said with as much cheer as she could muster.

Emily still said nothing.

Concerned, Jess gently lowered the comic book and met the girl's eyes. "You should eat, sweetheart."

Ignoring her advice, Emily laid the comic book down and asked, "Do you think they'll pay? The money, I mean…do you think mommy and daddy will pay to get me back?"

Jess sighed. "Oh honey, of *course* they will. A girl like you, they'd pay *ten times* the amount to get back."

"A girl like me?"

"Yes, Emily…a girl like you. Beautiful, smart, gentle…any parent would give their world to have a daughter like you."

"You really think so?"

"I *know* so, Emily."

"Would you?"

Jess frowned. "Would I what?"

"Give your world to have a kid like me?"

Jess smiled sadly. "You have *no* idea, angel. If I had a little girl, I'd want her to be *exactly* like you. Down to the last hair on her head."

"You're very nice," Emily said quietly. "Not like the others…"

"They're not so bad. The man who ruffled your hair…he's a real nice guy. The big woman, too. She's very kind. She looks a little scary and she shouts instead of speaking, but it's never in anger. The other man, the one who rode in back, he's just a mean old grump. Don't you pay him any mind, sweetheart."

Emily shrugged her shoulders, a childish gesture that amused Jess, then she eyed the sandwich. While she did so, Jess found her attention drawn to the window. In her absence, the girl had opened it a little and the cool breeze sneaking through felt very refreshing. She watched as the faded curtains swayed gently in the whispering wind and wondered how things were going out there for Curt.

He'll be fine.

Stay calm and it will all work out. Have faith, Jess.

Have faith.

She turned back to find Emily already munching on a ham-and-cheese sandwich. It seemed the girl had grown tired of *Superman* and, while eating, had already picked out her next comic-book. This one featured a character on the front whom Jess didn't recognize; someone or something by the name of *Swamp Thing*. The character looked fearsome. The artwork, however, was beautiful.

"They won't do it, you know." said Emily, quietly.

Jess, confused, asked, "Who won't do what, honey?"

"They won't do what you want."

"Who?" Jess asked, perplexed. "Your mommy and daddy?"

"Yeah."

"They won't do what…? Pay to get you back?"

"Nope."

Jess frowned. "Now why on earth would you think that?"

"Just because…"

Jess' heart ached for the girl.

How could she think such a thing?

"Don't even think that way for a *second*, honey. They're your parents. They love you more than you'll ever know. I promise you…they'll pay."

Emily stared at Jess. In the girl's eyes, she saw no hint of pain, only a weary acceptance. "They won't pay, Jess. I know it."

She said your name again.

It wasn't your imagination!

"Emily…I want to ask you something, okay?"

"Sure."

"Could you tell me why you keep calling me 'Jess'?"

The girl opened her comic, allowing her gaze to be drawn into its world. "It's your name, isn't it?"

Jess felt her stomach flip over on itself. "I don't…when did you hear anyone call me that?"

Emily ignored her. "They hate me, Jess. They hate me and they wish I was dead."

Jess dropped the question of identity, shocked by the child's steadfast insistence that her parents somehow hated her. Her mind swimming in fresh confusion, Jess asked, "Why would they hate you?"

"They don't *want* to hate me. Just like I don't want to hate the things I hate, like being alone, or the sound of thunder. They can't *help* hating me, though. They can't help how they feel."

"Darling, that's…"

"You'll see soon enough." Emily's eyes scanned the first pages of the comic. "They won't even answer the phone…"

7

Curt slammed the handset into the cradle, frustration twisting in his guts.

"Call again!" Pete shouted from the van. His voice sounded loud as thunder in the stillness of the night.

Curt winced. "Keep the noise down!"

Pete snorted. "Who the fuck is going to hear us all the way out here?"

The asshole has a point.

Curt knew he was being irrational. They were all alone out here. The only lights came from their own vehicle and from the cold moon above. There were no signs of headlights anywhere east, west, north or south. This part of the Mojave was a ghost world, especially at night.

Yet still…

The feeling had crept up on him as he'd inserted the coins into the phone and began dialing; the feeling that he was being watched, that eyes pregnant with malicious intent were studying him from somewhere out there among the Joshua trees, the Asters and the Saltbushes - calculating, waiting, seething with anticipation.

There's no one out there, dickhead.

It's just your imagination playing tricks on you.

But what if…?

There isn't. *Take a damn knee and get your head on straight. It's all going to go to plan.*

Then why the hell is no one answering the phone?

He tried to ignore the tumbling sensation in his guts and re-dialed, taking extra care to ensure he dialed the number exactly as it was written down.

The line connected. Again.

He waited. Again.

A minute passed while he shuffled from foot to foot, eying the darkness that engulfed him on all sides, listening to the unanswered connection-tone ringing in his ears like funereal bells, stark and dreadful.

Two minutes passed, feeling more like ten, as sweat began trickling down his forehead from his hairline and into his eyes, stinging them. He blinked them away, smoothing his hair back over his head.

Three minutes passed.

Shit!

They're not going to answer.

He looked back at the van, where Pete sat, frowning.

"What the fuck is going on?" Pete demanded.

"I don't know."

"Is it ringing?"

"Yes! Are you *sure* this is the right number?" Curt asked, angrily. "If you screwed this fucking thing up, Pete…" He warned.

"I didn't screw up *nothin'*! I checked and double-checked. Lisa did, too. That number you're holding there in your hand is the home number, man, guaranteed. I swear it."

"Well there's no god damn answer!"

"You gave the girl's nanny the right information, right? The time, the place?" Pete asked.

"You were *there*, Pete. You know I did."

"Fuck…I wonder if…nah." Pete said slowly, his unfinished thought infuriating Curt.

"What? Spit it the fuck out, Pete!"

"I was just thinking…maybe the nanny never made it back to the girl's parents."

Panic was beginning to dull Curt's ability to handle the situation. He was a mechanic, for Christ's sake, not a hardened criminal. They'd all been so fucking naïve…so *sure* this would go smoothly.

All but Jess.

What if Pete was onto something? What if something *had* happened to the girl's nanny on the way back to the family residence? She'd been shocked, dealt a terrible fright, and was no doubt in a state of heightened anxiety when she'd gotten back in her car and made for the girl's home residence. They'd smashed her mobile to ensure she did nothing rash, like immediately calling the cops when they'd sped off with the child, but that didn't mean she hadn't taken any action alone.

Alerted someone.

Called the cops from another phone.

Anything.

They had no *idea* what the nanny might do.

Hell, she could have crashed her car and died with the information still trapped inside her crushed skull, for all they knew.

They'd been careless. They hadn't covered every base. Now they might pay for it.

That's because you're supposed to be back home in Cider Creek, fixing up trucks, repairing windshields, replacing engines. Same with this asshole you're riding with. And your sister...she should be home with her kid, watching Jaws *for the hundredth time while the little guy whoops and hollers at the giant shark.*

Don't even think *about Jess.*

She didn't even want to be here.

There was no choice, another voice argued, within him.

No choice at all.

Again, that sensation of being watched laid its icy hand on his shoulder. In his mind, Curt perceived baleful eyes studying him from out there, amidst the dust and the darkness.

He listened a little longer, barely hearing the dial-tone over the sound of his own blood rushing through his veins.

Nothing.

"*Fuck!*" Curt slammed the phone down onto the cradle again.

A thought crept into his mind from the shadows of his burgeoning dread. There was another possible reason the girl's parents weren't answering the phone...

One other possibility, besides the nanny being lain dead in a ditch somewhere, or sat in a local police department, spilling her guts out...

The thought held, latching onto his psyche.

What if the girl's parents just didn't *want* to answer?

Curt pictured them, sat there on the other end of the line, listening to the shrill ringing of the phone, doing their very best to ignore it, hands clasped together, lips tight, eyes narrowed.

No. It was ridiculous.

No parent would forsake their child like that.

Would they?

The very idea was insane.

Curt pushed the thought from his mind as best he could, back down to that primal place where a man's irrational fears bubbled and churned. He wiped off the handset and the dialing buttons, then made his way back to

38

the van. He climbed into the driver's seat and sat there, lost for words, feeling utterly impotent.

"Now what?" Pete asked.

Curt barely heard him. He was too far adrift in his own dread-laced thoughts.

Think, man…think.

We take the kid back. Drop her off someplace, close to where we found her. Someplace safe.

But then, what about Jess?

Without the money, Jess would surely…

No!

This is going ahead.

We just need to think of a new way to contact the parents.

"We're heading back," he said flatly, keying the ignition.

"And then what?"

Curt spun the van around and put his foot down. His heart ached, knowing he'd soon have to relay this new situation to his wife.

"Then we recalibrate, Pete. We *think* of something. Something must have happened to the nanny. All we need to do is…"

Pete interrupted, echoing Curt's own deeply disturbing notion. "What if they *heard* the phone and just didn't answer?"

Again, Curt tried hard to convince himself the idea was insane. No parent would allow their child to suffer unduly.

It was unthinkable.

The van sped on through the suffocating blackness, heading back to the old house, where Jess and Lisa waited for him, along with one strange little girl who seemed to feel no fear.

Curt hit the gas.

8

Jess sat by Lisa at the table, cradling a hot mug of coffee and wondering how to express her concerns without appearing like a crazy person. Lisa was a trusted friend, but she was also aware of the pressures that Jess battled daily, always fighting to stay on top and keep her spirits high.

She didn't want to cause her friend undue worry about her mental health with everything *else* that was going on.

Jess tried to tell herself that her fears were nothing, merely the product of a tired mind.

After all, the strain of the day must surely be taking its toll on her. Not only on her steadily weakening body, but on her psyche, too. Emotionally, she was worn down to the nub. It was no small thing, doing what they'd all done. Despite their very best intentions and having absolutely no desire to harm the little girl in any way, the act of kidnapping itself had been terrible. No parent should ever have to experience what the poor girl's parents would be going through right at that very moment.

If they're going through anything at all, a small voice retorted from somewhere within her psyche.

That was nonsense, though. The girl had no way of knowing the goings-on outside the weathered walls of the large house and even if her relationship with her parents *was* strained in some way, (and how strained could relationships with an eight-year-old girl be?), no parent would ever forego their child's safety when they had the means to prevent it. The ransom may have been a lot of money to Jess and Curt, but to Emily's family, it was little more than chump-change.

So why was it eating away at her so?

Perhaps it was to do with the fact that the child also spoke Jess' name and did so with the same certainty that she condemned her parents. She *could* have overheard it at some point, yes, but Jess was sure her name hadn't been uttered above a whisper. The girl's room was locked up tight, was situated quite a distance from the kitchen where they'd based themselves. First there was the long hallway, then the staircase and from there the bedroom, locked up tight.

No *way* she could hear a whisper from up there.

Emily had her window open, but the bedroom was located at the rear of the house, positioning her far from traveling sound. You could swing a cat in the place and no one would hear it screaming, so unless the kid had superhuman hearing like the characters in her comics, then there really seemed to be no way she could have picked it up.

And then there was Emily's behavior...

She was a delightful girl without question, if a little withdrawn. Under everyday circumstances her calm, collected demeanor would be admirable, but given the highly stressful events the girl had endured in the last five or so hours, it all seemed a little...off.

Maybe you are *overtired, Jess. Maybe you really are.*

Feeling the familiar burning in her throat, Jess reached for a handkerchief. She placed it to her mouth and allowed the painful, hacking cough to find release. Though her eyes were closed as the latest coughing fit took hold, she knew Lisa was watching her from across the table, silently worrying herself to death.

When the fit was over, she quickly folded the handkerchief, concealing the expelled blood in its folds.

"I can see it on your lips, you know?" Lisa said.

Jess frowned.

"The blood. It's...it's on your lips."

"Shit."

Jess quickly wiped the back of her hand across her lips. Sure enough, her hand came away red.

"Why don't you go lie down? There are plenty of rooms up there. Pick one and get some rest. I can look after the girl."

Not yet able to speak, Jess shook her head. She took a moment to catch her breath. "No...no, I'm okay...I need to do this, Lisa. We all have to do our part in this and I have a good bond with her. She trusts me, I think. Things are tough on that little girl, Lisa. No need to mix things up and make them any tougher."

Lisa leaned forward. "You look tired, Jess. *Real* tired. Won't do any of us any good, having you collapse on us with all this shit going on."

"I'll be fine, honestly. The coughing fits...they come and go."

"I know they come and go, but they've been 'coming' a lot more than 'going' since you demanded to take part in this. I thought you were against it. Curt told me as much."

"I had to be here, Lisa. I had to."

"Why?" Lisa asked. She lowered her head. "Don't bother answering that. I already know...your unwavering sense of responsibility, right?"

"Something like that, yes."

"Let me tell you something, Jess...just because this is *for* you, doesn't mean it needed to *involve* you."

"I know...it's not just that, it's..."

"What?"

"It's the girl."

"What about her?"

"I wanted to be here for her when she, you know, went through all this."

"You don't even *know* her."

"Doesn't matter. She's a child. She needs me here. She needs someone who can care for her and soothe her. She needs..."

"You're not her mother, Jess."

"I know that!" Jess barked back with more venom than she intended. She took pause, breathed deep. "I'm sorry. I just...I wanted to get to know her. In a strange way, when you lay all the cards on the table, she's the one who, if this all works out, will be saving my life."

Lisa sat back in her chair. The wood creaked under her ample frame, threatening to succumb. For the moment, it held firm, if only just.

"Jessica, you have a heart of purest gold and I love you for it. I really do."

"But?"

"But while your heart is top of the line, your brain could use a little work, girl, if you don't mind me saying so."

Jess laughed softly. Lisa joined her, killing the tension in the room instantaneously.

"You might be right, at that," Jess agreed, raising her coffee to her lips now that the coughing fit was evidently over.

She took a sip. Pain followed the warm coffee down her throat. Placing the mug on the kitchen table, Jess tried to hock up some of the phlegm. It hurt like hell to do so, but she did her best to hide her pain.

Lisa had seen enough pain in her life without watching her friend wither and die like grapes untended on the vine.

Pulling out a fresh handkerchief, she spat the offending chunk of pinkish muck into it and folded. Catching her breath, she said. "I know you'll think that what I'm about to say *also* has something to do with my brain needing a tune-up, but...I think there's something strange going on, Lisa."

Lisa's soft smile fell away, replaced by a puzzled frown. "Strange? Strange how?"

"It could be nothing. Probably *is* nothing, but there was something Emily said upstairs. About her parents."

Lisa was all ears. "What did she say about them, Jess? Talk to me, honey. And don't worry about me thinking you're nuts. I *already* think you're crazy as a badger in a bag...so spill it."

Jess still had no idea how to word her disquiet, so she simply blurted her concerns out. "She...Emily...she said that her parents won't answer the phone when Curt and Pete make the call."

Lisa huffed, "Now why in the hell wouldn't they answer?"

Jess spoke quietly. "She said they...well...she said they *hate* her."

Lisa smiled. It was an understanding smile, one full of kindness. "Jess, that's just the fears inside of a scared little girl making themselves known. She probably feels they've abandoned her, left her to the big bad wolves. You got to understand, when anything painful or stressful happens to a child of her age - and *especially* one who's lived such a sheltered life, locked away from the world most days in that golden palace they call a 'home', the child is going to feel betrayed. They may not have the self-awareness or the vocabulary to express it properly. They may not even know they feel that way themselves. But they do, darlin'. They do. For a kid like her...fresh to this world and having seen so little of it...the simplest change to their daily pattern can cut the legs right out from under them. And when those legs get cut out and the kid topples over, who do you think they come crying to? Who do you think they blame?"

"Their parents."

"That's right! Their parents. And those cries aren't fueled by hurting alone, honey. They're fueled by *anger, resentment,* and sometimes even *hate.* Hell, the number of times I've had little Billy holler at me like I'm the very Devil himself, popped up from Hell! He's called me every name under the sun, that boy, leastways the ones he's *allowed* to call me. You'd think me the worst damned mother who ever walked God's blessed lands, Jess. I swear it."

Jess laughed, though her unease remained.

"Yeah, he's a little spitfire."

"You know it, honey. You damn sure know it."

Jess frowned. "I guess you're right. It's probably nothing."

Lisa spoke quietly and with love. "This isn't about something…else…is it, sweetheart?"

Despite Lisa' reluctance to voice her concerns, it was clear what her sister-in-law was referring to.

She was referring to Petra.

She thinks this is about her.

Isn't everything, though, when it comes right down to it, Jess?

The thought of her was enough to conjure bitter tears.

Painful as Lisa's allusions were, they rang true.

But Jess wasn't ready to fully admit such things.

Not yet.

Not to herself and not to the others, whether true or not.

"No. No, Lisa. It's nothing. I'm just a little jittery, I think. It'll pass. I'm sorry."

"There's nothing to be sorry *for*, darlin'. Not one single thing. This'll all be over soon enough and you and Curt will be far gone from here. Once you guys get the cash, you can both start a new life together, someplace over the border, away from all this shit."

"A fresh start…"

"It surely will be, at that."

"Thanks, Lisa."

"Sometimes when you're running, Jess, it ain't got nothin' to do with being afraid."

Jess fought back the tears, unwilling to let her friend see just how close she may have come to nailing the root cause of her concerns. "You know," she said, amused even in her grief, "For a crazy old bird from the desert, you're quite the accomplished psychiatrist."

Lisa's laughter was full-throated and warm. When the big, kind woman laughed with such abandon, her breasts jiggled like two bowls of

Jell-O. "I ain't just a pretty face and a tight body, sister!" she exclaimed. "Now, where the *hell* have my brother and that dipshit, rat-bastard I call an 'ex-husband' gotten to?"

9

Alone in the bedroom, Emily was lost in the comic's world, enthralled by the hero's selflessness, mesmerized by their kindness and nobility. She scanned the pages with eyes on fire, drinking up the intricately drawn artwork, bathing in the story being spun.

She wished *she* could be a superhero, taking on the evils of the world, protecting the innocent from the darkness that permeated their lives. That would be a wonderful life. A better life. If she had the powers of *Wonder Woman,* or *Thor,* she'd fight to make the world a better place. A safe place. She'd be the best superhero of them all and do good for the whole world.

But to do good, you have to be *good,* she thought, sadly.

She wanted to be good. As good as a girl could be. She always had.

But she was still only a little girl, an eight-year-old kid with an eight-year old's temperament and understanding of heroism.

There had been sacrifices in Emily's life, some of which still burned at her burgeoning sense of worth. Her grandmother, for instance. And her Uncle Harvey. Those had been bad times. Terrible times.

She'd done what she had to do, though.

Not all good people could be saved, it was true, but not all evil went unpunished, either. There was *some* justice in the world, at least.

Uncle Harvey...what had happened to him...*that* had been justice. She was young, but old enough to understand that the affections of an older person could be twisted into something darker.

Her uncle's fate, Emily found easy to live with.

Her grandmother, though.

That had been an accident. A terrible one.

Emily's heart lurched as the memories flooded her. She felt a sickness swirl in her tummy.

In her mind, she saw the tall dark impossible figure that had taken her grandmother. A cruel and twisted mockery of the kind old lady's beloved and cherished Jesus.

Granny had loved the man. Every room of her home had a framed picture of him, long hair and beard flowing, blue-eyes shining with eternal kindness, a slight smile, knowing and wise, etched on his face. He hung on crosses in Granny's bedroom, held a lamb in a painting in the kitchen. In every image, he looked so compassionate.

He hadn't looked like that when he came for her Granny.

He hadn't looked like that at all.

Sometimes, Emily could still hear Granny's screams, echoing in the corridors of her mind.

Though the screams hadn't been the worst part.

The worst part had been the terror on her grandmother's face; the horrible expression of fear etched there as the black and corrupt version of her hero loomed over her, his once warm and loving eyes now burning with hatred and lust, his smile no longer that of a comforting companion, but a hungry, leering grin.

Stop! She demanded of herself. *You were only a baby. How were you to know what would happen? You were innocent.*

So was Granny.

Emily closed her eyes. She tried to remember her Granny as she'd been before it came for her. Instead, she saw nothing. Only distant screams filled the darkness behind her eyes.

The room's silence fed the memory. Emily cursed it.

She wished she could hear them moving downstairs, or hear what they were saying. In a house so large, filled with long corridors and countless bedrooms, dining rooms and secret places, sound traveled, but not so far that she could hear it. Just to listen to them speak…to dull the sounds from her past, that haunted her so…

Sadly, unlike *Superman,* super-hearing wasn't within her power.

Emily's powers lay elsewhere.

And there was nothing *super* about them.

She opened her eyes and focused on the comic, savoring the magic, inked there by unseen hands. As she stared determinedly at the colorful adventure, she grew steadily more aware of the subtle shifts in light; shadows stretching their dark limbs across the walls and the ceiling, as the moon glided slowly through the skies outside her room.

Night approached.

It was her favorite time.

It was the *perfect* time for using what power she *did* possess, though often it seemed her power was using *her*.

47

Fear was always at its most potent when experienced in the night-time.

She stared down at the comic's artwork.

On the page, Swamp Thing was locked in a life-or-death battle with a black, slimy monster of some kind. Mud covered his muscular, monstrous frame. In the background, a woman screamed from her hiding spot behind a tree, of a sort Emily could not name.

Emily stared at the monster the hero wrestled with, all tentacles and teeth, hunger and claws. She understood the artist had sought to create something fearsome for the *Swamp Thing* to battle, but the monster in the comic wasn't frightening at all. Not to her.

Though fear, she knew all too well, was subjective.

The terror on the brightly colored page couldn't hold a candle to the thing that had taken Granny. Or the nightmare that had put a stop to Uncle Harvey's evil…

And besides, why be jealous or afraid of a superhero's abilities or a villain's strengths? It was all make-believe. It was fun to imagine such things existing, but there was no pure magic in the real world, not of the sort dreamt of by fanciful artists and writers of cartoons.

None of that was real.

The things living inside a person's heart, though…the unique terrors that lurked, deep down inside the souls, of every man, woman and child…*those* were real.

Very real.

For a time, anyway.

Until those fears ate the person alive.

As Emily understood it, fear was like a disease. It fed and fed and fed until there was nothing left to feed on, then it died in the embrace of its host.

The host and its fear became one.

Forever

Suddenly bored with the comic, Emily turned to watch the moon grinning from the night sky. She enjoyed the feel of its radiance on her skin. It calmed her somehow.

The woman calmed her, too.

Jess.

She would be returning soon, Emily was sure. The sandwiches had been nice and all, but she much preferred the company of Jess to any sandwich, however tasty.

She knew that Jess would have come back quicker if she could, but Emily understood that she was very busy. When close to the kind lady, she could sense the fear housed within. It clung to Jess' skin like a sweat, inspired not by the searing desert heat but by a nagging sense of anxiety, brought on by what she and her friends had done; bringing Emily here to this old, run-down place where no one could find them.

And alongside fear, Jess felt remorse.

Emily could sense that, too.

She could sense a whole lot of things.

She liked Jess, despite the woman's mistakes. She liked her a lot.

She'll be back soon, she comforted herself.

All Emily had to do was wait.

She allowed herself to relax, put down the comic still held loosely in her hands and laid back on the bed. As she let herself drift and let her body sink into the comfortable bedsheets, she allowed the ghost of her grandmother to fade away like morning mist under the sun, and, rather than dwell on what couldn't be changed, Emily turned her inner eye towards the terrors she could taste on the souls of the women downstairs. With terrible fascination she explored their dread.

It hurt to do so.

She had no trust for the big woman and tasting her fear was easily manageable, but Jess…

Jess was nice. Really nice.

Emily hoped it was enough to save her.

10

Curt glanced at Pete as he cracked another bottle open. His third in the short time since they'd left behind the phone-booth, and with it their control of the situation.

Pete was staring straight ahead, eyes growing blearier by the minute. Shadows flitted across his stubbled features as he held the bottle aloft and guzzled down the contents in one go.

"You said you'd stop drinking about five beers back..."

Pete afforded Curt a wolfish grin. "What are you, my fucking *mother*?"

"We need you thinking straight."

Curt winced as the bottle clunked to the van's floor. It rolled under the passenger seat to join the rest of the discarded beer-bottles.

Pete was openly sneering now. "And just why the *fuck* would I want to stay straight, Curt? Tell me. I'm all ears. Seems to me from where I'm sitting, being '*clear-headed*' has gotten us absolutely fucking nowhere! I think the time for good behavior has passed, amigo, don't you?"

"It's not over yet, Pete. We need to keep it together."

"Not over!? Curt...they didn't answer the fucking *phone*! They've gone to the law and are hatching a plan *right this fucking minute*!"

"If they went to the law, they'd have advised them to answer the phone, Pete. They wouldn't risk the girl's life on a gamble like that."

"How the fuck would you know what they would and wouldn't do? You workin' for the feds, now?"

"Fuck you."

"Yeah, fuck me."

Curt was shaken, there was no denying it, but Pete's faulty logic only rattled him further. The feds *would* have had the parents answer. They'd have stalled for time. Tried to pinpoint the location of the girl. The phone would *not have* wrung out.

Which means...

It had played over and over in his mind; a broken vinyl on a record-player, spinning onwards and onwards, pumping fear instead of music directly to his heart.

They didn't care.

Crazy as it sounded, and it did sound off-the-wall fucking insane, Emily's parents didn't care enough to take the call.

Pete cracked another bottle-top with his cigarette lighter. Curt watched as it spun through the air in front of him and hit the van's front window. Pete wore a lop-sided grin. The booze, regardless of his familiarity with its effects, was beginning to take hold.

"We should turn the van around, Curt," Pete said flatly.

Curt glanced again at Pete. "What the hell are you talking about, 'turn the van around?' Why?"

"You *know* why…"

"No, Pete, I don't. So how about you fucking fill me in!? We going to go back there and call again? What the hell for!?"

Pete spoke quietly and with a steady, considered tone. "All I'm saying is, we should reconsider our options." He waved his hand between Curt and himself. "You and me, I mean. The *two* of us."

Curt rubbed his eyes. A headache was looming on his horizon, a motherfucker set to hurtle him into a world of hurt. Pete's bullshit wasn't helping.

"What are you saying, Pete? Spit it the fuck out, will you?"

Pete took a deep breath; whether feigning guilt or compassion, Curt couldn't be sure. Whichever it was, the performance didn't work. Pete was incapable of either. It made Curt think of the pod people from that old 50's flick, *Invasion of the Body Snatchers*.

"Look," Pete implored, "for all we know, the cops are hunting for us already. The fucking nanny could have panicked, bypassed the family and went straight to the law."

"We wore masks."

"So-fucking-*what*!?"

"They have no idea who we are, where we're headed, or what we're planning to do!"

Pete chuckled. "I've seen enough movies to know that if the pigs are involved in a ransom situation, you either end up staring through iron bars, with a dick up your ass for the rest of your life, or you spend your final moments bleeding out from a hundred bullets in a pool of your own blood. Fuck *both* those choices, Curt! Fuck 'em *both*!"

Curt rubbed his eyes, gritted his teeth, tried hard to concentrate.

51

"We should just *go*," Pete said quietly, controlling himself momentarily. "We can be over the border by daybreak. You and me, Curt. The two of us. We did our best, but we can't handle this shit, man. You know it and I know it."

Curt agreed.

They *couldn't* handle this 'shit'.

But there was no manhunt going on out there, amidst the cacti and the dust.

There *was* a girl, though…a fragile, innocent girl whose parents had somehow turned their back on her. He sensed their paternal betrayal in every molecule of his being.

The dull, incessant beat of the burgeoning headache thrummed behind Curt's eyes. He tried to ignore it, to will it away.

"There's no god damn manhunt going on, Pete. For God's sake, think!"

"I'm telling you, there is!"

"There isn't! We need to head back and think of another plan."

"No fucking way."

"What about Lisa, Pete? She's the mother of your son. If you believe the law are onto us, are you just gonna leave her out there at that house, to wait for the authorities to catch up to her? Jesus Christ, she could be killed! At the very least, she'll do serious time. That something you can live with, Pete?"

Pete lowered his chin to his chest, puffing out air. His movements were steadily morphing into those of a drunk, sluggish and exaggerated. "I think so, yeah. I think I *can* live with it. Better that shit than going back to prison…"

"What about Billy, huh? What about your son?"

"I never see the little shit these days, anyway. What the fuck do I care?"

Curt gripped the steering wheel tight. His knuckles turned white as he fought to maintain composure. "You're a real piece of work, buddy, you know that?" he said, through gritted teeth.

Pete surprised him by giggling. It sounded hollow, bitter. "You just figuring that out, Curt? Not too quick off the mark, are you?"

"I've been good to you, Pete."

"Yeah, yeah."

"All these years I've been the best friend I could be, for my sister's sake and for the sake of that '*little* shit', as you call him…Billy."

"*Fuck* your sister! We're looking at twenty to twenty-five years and you're concerned about *that* dumb bitch!?"

Curt felt the leather of the steering wheel grind into his palms, burning. "I'm warning you, Pete…"

"In case you missed the fucking memo, you're no longer my fucking boss. You don't get to warn me about anything anymore, you got that…*pal*?" Pete sneered. He was slurring his words now, quickly deteriorating.

"We're going back to the house, asshole. Even if we *can't* get the ransom, we're not leaving my family back there."

"Why the fuck not!? Your sister is a lost cause, Curt, and in case you hadn't noticed, without that ransom money poor little Jess will, well…"

Curt swallowed his fury and tried to focus on the road ahead as it rushed toward him.

Pete laid a hand on his shoulder in a disgusting gesture of camaraderie. Curt felt bile rise in his throat and recoiled at the other man's touch. He could smell the stale beer on Pete's breath as his one-time employee moved closer.

"I know you two sweethearts are keeping the cards close to your chests as to what's going on with her and I don't much give a shit, to be honest." Pete paused for a second. "It's cancer, though, right? It's always fucking cancer, man. That shit only ends one way without treatment, good buddy, and even then…"

"Don't you fucking say it!" Curt warned.

"Say what? That she's *definitely* gonna die without the money? It's the truth, ain't it? Might as well just leave her behind and take a load off, Curt."

Whether it was the alcohol puppeteering Pete or another example of the man's utter lack of empathy, it didn't matter.

Curt's world became a red haze. The road rushing toward him, a blood-red tsunami. He felt it bare down on him, eager to drown him in its fury.

The vicious drunken bastard was right.

Without the money, Jess wouldn't survive the coming year.

A vision flashed before his eyes – *Jess, laying in a hospital bed, her eyes swollen red with the expulsion of bitter tears, dull with the weariness of erosion, her will spent completely, her fight extinguished while all around her, doctors loom like terrible black angels over one already dead. Her life is leaking out right before his eyes, ebbing from her pale form as she gasps and sputters and breathing becomes a memory.*

From all around him the sounds of the cold machines bleeping and whirring, drowning out the weakening murmurs of his poor, dying sweetheart. He screams at the doctors to do something...ANYTHING...while the only woman he's ever loved, begins to fade before his very eyes; her inner light growing dimmer, dimmer, dimmer...

She tries to word something around bloodied lips, but can't form the words. Her body rattles, her muscles, what's left of them, tighten momentarily, then loosen. Her bowels release in a final moment of indignity. The room fills with the smell of fresh shit, but Curt only smells death. Her death, his death, the death of everything.

"Turn the fucking car around!" Pete growled. Suddenly, his hands were grasping for the steering wheel. Curt clawed at Pete's fingers, loosening his grip.

"What the hell are you doing!?" Curt screamed, panic overriding his rage.

"Stop the fucking car!" Pete roared. The car veered wildly, left and right, swaying from one side of the dirt road to the next. Dust kicked up around the open window, near-blinding Curt as Pete lunged forward.

"Stop the fucking car!" Pete roared again.

Curt hit the brakes.

The whole crazy moment had lasted less than ten seconds, but it was too late. The van spun out of control and Curt's world became one of madly spinning lights, screams and the deafening screech of tires. The van upturned, hurtling down a sharp ravine like a discarded toy. Metal squealed and bent, windows shattered, something in his arm snapped, followed by a white-hot, all-engulfing agony, that washed his senses away, filling his world with pain. Screaming, he watched helplessly as the side window rushed toward him in slow motion. He felt it connect with his face, felt the sickening crunch, but only briefly.

Then all was dark.

Curt fell deep into yet another ravine somewhere within his mind, while phantom cries of his dying wife followed.

11

Jess climbed the staircase slowly, using the old wooden bannister to balance herself as she moved up the steps. One by one, the stairs creaked and yawned beneath her weight, conjuring thoughts of old horror films – old dark houses, thunder storms and sealed, cobwebbed rooms that held deep dark secrets.

The upper landing was dark, lit only by the small strip of light emanating from the room where the girl resided.

She studied the light beneath the door as she ascended, taking solace in it. Still, the sense of the uncanny, that had gripped her since her previous visit to the girl, held tight.

The talk with Lisa, while rational and adult, obviously hadn't done the trick. At least not fully. The shadows played tricks on her, forming patterns and shapes in the dark that chilled her to the bone. Why was it that when the mind birthed images from shadow, they were almost universally insidious?

Jess felt like a child, rising from the soft sanctuary of her bed late at night, braving the quiet and the murk as she slowly, carefully, made her way to the bathroom, with its warm, safe light and its thick oak door.

Only this time, it was the light that caused her pause. It was the secrets held behind the old oak door that raised her heartbeat and made her palms sweat.

And it made Jess feel terrible.

She liked the child immensely, having warmed to the sweet-natured Emily right off the bat, but the things she'd said and the way she'd said them...

Something was wrong. Something was very wrong.

Something is *wrong, Jess...with* you.

God damn it...go in there and look after her.

A war seemed to be playing out inside of her. On one side, there was the caring, maternal and loving side that found the girl to be everything Jess had once hoped for in a child of her own. On the other side, a primal instinct; something ancient and devolved that feared, took pause and bristled.

A thought entered Jess' head that terrified her more than a child's demonic imaginings ever could. What if her mind was already deteriorating? What if the final stages had already begun and her rationale was already crumbling?

Jess closed her eyes and rubbed them, trying to shake off the growing exhaustion she felt, determined not to succumb to the irrational fear, surely a symptom of the churning concoction of deteriorating health and strength, physical and emotional.

Lisa was right. There was nothing off about the girl. She was simply a sweet, open-hearted child being put through a traumatic experience. Outwardly calm, but no doubt tore up inside at having been stolen from her safe, secure, insular world.

Jess opened her eyes again and watched the sliver of light pushing out from within the girl's room.

Nothing to fear but fear itself, wasn't that what they said?

Soft laughter came from within the room.

It was Emily.

"People are scared by the silliest things sometimes," Emily sounded amused, *entertained* even, as she talked to herself.

A cold dread twisted around Jess' heart, indefinable.

What's she doing in there?

She's a little kid, Jess. She's keeping her mind busy.

Who's she addressing?

An imaginary friend?

Someone else?

Get a hold on this shit, Jess, she's talking to herself. She's probably traumatized and taking solace in her imagination; it's what kids do.

Go up there and open the god damn door.

Jess heard something else.

Something chitinous, inhuman, cold.

She froze halfway up the staircase, her whole body grew rigid, her eyes never leaving the sliver of light at the foot of the door.

Beneath the door, Jess saw movement.

Shadows, rushing past, one then another, then another, as whatever was inside the room with Emily moved across the floor.

And it moved fast.

Jess gasped, covering her mouth to mask the sound.

Inside the room, Emily giggled, delighted.

Jess stood rooted to the spot, two stairs from the upper landing. In her chest, her heart thundered.

She held her breath.

More sounds from within – a series of soft thumps, something heavy, landing on the carpet. It sounded like the scuttling of many legs.

"How could anyone be afraid of you?" Emily asked aloud.

Something was in the room…something other than little Emily.

Whatever it was, it was big. Big as a dog, at least.

Realization crashed into Jess. Shame followed, though there was no time to allow its needles to prick.

It had to be an animal of some sort!

It must have gotten in through the window.

"Shit!" Jess exclaimed.

The ice thawing in her veins, her body free from terror's rigor mortis and fueled now by the need to protect the precious child, Jess tore up the remaining stairs two at a time.

Frantic, she reached for the key in the latch and turned it as, beneath the door, the shadows danced.

12

Lisa, sat alone by the kitchen table, smoking. She inhaled the nicotine deeply, savoring its acrid taste on her tongue. It had been two months since she'd lit up and tasted that sweet nectar. She'd couldn't bring herself – even when the craving took hold – to try those 'vaporizers' or whatever the kids were calling them. For one thing, they looked dumb as all hell with those silly little lights popping on and off at the end, as though aflame. The hell with that. For another, she'd heard how dangerous they could be. She'd heard horror stories in the papers and from friends about the damn things blowing up in people's faces, burning their eyes out.

She winced as she pictured it – a face, skin melting, eyes seared from the skull, bright teeth shining from black, charred lips.

No, to hell with that.

It wasn't a whole lot more appealing a fate than lung cancer.

If she was going to quit, she'd damn well *quit*.

The end. Full stop. No half measures.

And she'd been doing well, too, up until tonight.

If that bastard, Pete, hadn't left a packet sat right there *in front of me on the table*, she rued.

But that wasn't fair. There was no one to blame but herself. She'd let the stress get to her and the more time that passed, the deeper she felt herself acquiesce to the pressure.

She'd done her best to keep Jess calm. She needed to stay as level as possible. Any outward worry that Lisa displayed would do her sister-in-law no damn good, and could only lead to more complications. Lisa was a true believer in the concept that a healthy mind lent itself to a healthy body, and this whole cursed venture was in *no way* conducive to a healthy mind.

So, she'd stayed calm, kept her cool, did everything she could to ease Jess' fears regarding both the late return of Curt and Pete, and the supposedly strange, abnormal behavior of the child upstairs.

Jess had gone to check on the kid a few minutes ago, leaving Lisa alone to contemplate what she understood about the situation.

Images flashed before her mind.

Curt and Pete, held at gunpoint, ratted out by the nanny, pulled over by the roadside and dragged off to jail for ever more. Or dead, their heads blown off by trigger-happy law enforcement's gunfire, bits and pieces of their brains scattered across some forgotten highway in the devil's backyard.

And what of her? What if *she* was apprehended?

What would become of little Billy?

Another unwelcome movie flickered behind her eyelids.

Billy, scarred and traumatized by the incarceration of his mother, with nowhere to go. Fed through the production factory of the adoption system, taken in by outwardly kind and gentle adults, promised safety and shelter. All lies. Just a plaything for the twisted perversions of his keepers. Kept undernourished, filthy, his little body used to satiate every sick whim. Touched, probed, hurt...

The horrifying imagery seemed to spring from nowhere, fully formed. Such an extreme imagining - and one materialized from her own mind with no effort and no reasoning - shook her. The mind was a dark and terrible thing. The severity of Billy's imagined fate rattled her to the core.

Lisa wiped away tears she barely knew were there and took another drag on the cigarette with increasingly shaking fingers.

She wondered how Billy was doing at that moment. Was he thinking of her? Excited for her to come back to him? To take him home and love him and tell him bedtime stories and tuck him in, nice and warm and kiss his forehead goodnight?

Exhaling smoke that rode on trembling breath, Lisa upturned her wrist and studied her watch, staring impotently as her heart beat in time with the ticking of the clock.

Goddammit, Curt...where are you...?

13

Curt awoke to searing heat. He wondered if he'd died and found his way to Hell.

The first thing he felt was a crushing pressure on his chest, squeezing the air mercilessly from his lungs. Blood flowed into his eyes as his vision swam in and out of focus. Amidst the dark red shapes, he could see the bright light of flame; the dancing fire fractured and distorted through the prism of the shattered windshield. There was the whirring of wheels turning and, to his right, the metallic screech of the passenger door being forced open.

He tried to form words with bloodied lips, hoping to alert Pete to his condition. The words wouldn't come.

Fighting a rising panic, Curt struggled to make sense of his situation. He was upside down, held in place by the seatbelt. It coiled ever-tighter around his chest like a python around its prey, choking the life out of him, threatening to crush his ribs to splinters. Some may be broken already, but that was the least of his concerns. His vision was darkening, consciousness dimming in the agonizing grip of the safety belt.

Curt tried to move his right arm. Whatever meagre breath was left inside his body was expelled in a coughing, bloody, silent scream as pain seared his senses. Twisting his head around painfully, he looked at his arm and felt his horror grow tenfold.

The arm was twisted back on itself, just above the elbow. Blood spurted from the ragged flesh midway down his arm, welling around a jutting, splintered bone.

Crying now, he twisted his neck in the other direction, thankful that at least his spine somehow remained intact. His left arm - bruised near-black and hanging limp, seemed to be in far better shape than his right. He tried flexing his fingers, found that he could move them, then tried moving his whole arm, understanding that if he couldn't undo the seatbelt, the very thing that was designed to protect him would choke the life from his helpless, trapped body.

Moaning in agony, he raised his good arm. It took what felt like an eternity to get the damn thing up towards his chest, an eternity more to shakily locate the seatbelt's latch. When he found it Curt closed his eyes and prayed it was still operational. And then he pressed the button.

There was a soft click, a terror-stricken moment where it seemed to hold, then a short fall towards the upturned roof of the van, that brought fresh, mind-obliterating pain.

Landing hard on his right side, Curt finally found his scream.

Fighting to hold onto consciousness, he looked to the open passenger door. He could see very little besides the billowing black smoke and the reflection of flame from somewhere off to the right, where the passenger door was swung wide open.

No sign of Pete at all.

He began moving, slowly, shuffling along the van's upturned metal roof, while his right arm leaked blood below his waist, like a snail expelling slime as it slithered. The heat from the flames nearby was intensifying steadily. He smelled the hair on his arms burning as he clutched with his left hand at the metal rim of the open door, desperately trying to pull his broken body free of the wreck.

The whole vehicle would go up in flames at any second.

Wailing in pain, he grabbed onto the doorframe and pulled with all his might. Five seconds…ten…

He was going to cook alive inside this god forsaken van.

Bracing himself and taking a stinging breath that seemed to turn his throat to ash, Curt pulled with all his might.

Almost there.

Grateful for the years of hard labor that afforded him even the slightest hint of a chance, Curt focused on the doorway, removing himself as best as he could from the pain, the terror and the hellish heat that made the flesh on his arms tighten and crack.

He was almost out now.

Drooling and gibbering madly as the exposed bone rubbed against his jeans, grinding his mangled arm into the metal beneath, he pulled hard as he could. His vision faltered, blackness claimed him for the briefest moment. Curt felt almost thankful for it.

Then he was back in the here and now and the cruelty of it made him want to curse the gods.

Dammit, Curt…pull!

Having moved forward enough, he found he now could move his legs. Not much, but enough to perhaps help expel himself from the wreckage. Acrid smoke ripped at his eyeballs, crawled down his tortured throat and dulled his senses further. He could smell his hair begin to burn. It wouldn't be long now until he was burned alive.

Strength and will rapidly fading, Curt tensed his grip on the doorframe, dug his feet into the roof beneath as best he could, closed his eyes and kicked both legs against the scolding metal as he simultaneously pulled with his one still-useful arm.

Again, darkness, as solid and perfect as death, stole his vision.

"Jess", he wheezed. "I'm sorry."

There came a whooshing sound from his rear. Curt immediately felt the flames lick hungrily at his legs and prayed for the foul smoke to fully devour his senses, before the cruel flames found purchase.

As his strength ebbed to nearly nothing, he surrendered to his fate.

And then he saw Jess.

Still as stone. An open casket. Makeup unable to hide the erosion beneath; a hideous mannequin, cruelly mocking all that she'd been.

Curt pulled one last time.

And then...fresh air.

Blind and howling, Curt slid from the wreckage, felt the sweet, coarse kiss of the desert dust on his lips and with all he had left, he shuffled from death's bitter clutches.

He couldn't see the inferno to his rear as he rolled from the wreckage, but he could feel it on his tail.

He made it perhaps six feet from the van before flames engulfed the entire vehicle.

He made it a further three feet, before his limbs gave way. Curt slumped to the hard dirt and lost himself once more.

14

Pete limped on through the gathering night, followed by thoughts darker than any desert sky. He did what he could to ignore the pain in his skull, pushing it way down deep inside as he battled to focus his mind on the matter at hand.

Things had gotten pretty fucking heavy, pretty fucking quickly, but now wasn't the time to surrender to pain, nor was it a time for contemplation.

A part of his mind – the tiny part that strived to be decent and moral – niggled at his psyche as he formed his plan of action. He'd battled that side of himself for many years, hating its restrictions on his wants, needs and desires, resenting its nature, its ability to creep upon him in the small hours of the night and whisper insidiously, over and over…

You're a monster. You're a monster. You're a monster.

There'd been a lot of long nights filled with that same incessant whisperings in the wake of the things he'd done to his family, the things he'd put them through.

Lisa.

Billy…his only son.

No! Don't fucking think about it!

Not now!

It's done. It's done and it's over.

Pete blinked the blood from his eyes, trying to clear his line of sight. It was difficult enough seeing through the black haze of the mind-numbing headache that gripped his skull like an iron clamp.

How far out was he from the old house? It couldn't be far. It couldn't be more than maybe a mile now. He'd be there soon. Fuck his mangled leg. Fuck his split-open forehead and *fuck* that insistent poisonous voice inside his head that begged him not to cross this new line that he aimed to cross. The last line a man *could* cross.

Pete stopped to catch his breath, bending forward and placing his hands on his thighs. Sweat mixed with blood from the huge gash on his head and trickled down his face and chin, lighting up the many abrasions that carved up his face. He inhaled slowly, methodically, while he bled onto the cold, moonlight tarmac of the two-lane road.

He reached into his pocket for a smoke.

"Fuck!"

None there. He must have lost them when he crawled from the wreckage. Or when the van had overturned like some shit that happened in the fucking *Terminator* movies. That had been some serious shit, back there. No doubt about it. He'd made his way about two hundred yards from the twisted, smoking wreckage – marveling at his good fortune to be still whole, with two arms, two legs and a head - before spinning on his heels and waiting for the fireworks. It took a little time, but when the fireworks came and the vehicle lit up the endless blackness of the night with brilliant flame, he'd allowed himself a smile.

So long, Curt, ole buddy... see you on the other side, ya self-righteous prick.

Again, that tiny, near imperceptible voice in his mind whispered of betrayal, of loyalty, of humanity. It should have been rendered insignificant over the years, washed away by the things he'd done, but it persisted – a devil on his back, weighing him down.

Curt had been good to him. He'd been a friend - or as close to a friend as Pete had ever had - and he couldn't deny the tug of remorse that ate away at him as he watched the flames climb upwards to the sky.

You had no choice, hoss. No choice at all.

And he was *a self-righteous prick,* he thought, dulling the glimmer of guilt worming through him.

And it was true. Curt was one of the good guys. The sort of guy who'd pack an old ladies shopping for her, then drive her home if the rain came falling, whether it was on his way or not. The sort of guy who'd leave the bar early, alone and sober, unwilling to take advantage of the wasted young girls who could no more remember what you did to them when they slept than they could remember their first independent shit. Guys like Curt weren't cut out for what needed to be done back at the house.

That sort of work took a man whose will and whose instinct for survival was cast in stone. A man who could ignore the paltry charms of a clear conscience and do what had to be done to breathe free air.

A man like *Pete*.

Pete hawked up a bitter mixture of thick phlegm and blood. He spat it at his feet, disgusted. He closed his eyes tight, willing away the throbbing, miserable heartbeat of the migraine, and stood up straight.

Just a few more miles...just a few more motherfucking miles and we'll wrap this shit-show in a bow and send it down the river.

And then?

What then?

Then we make for the bright lights and firm titties of Mexico, never to be seen or heard from again.

Let's just get this shit done and be free of it.

Pete looked back over his shoulder. Off in the distance, a 'ways out from the road, the faintest glimmer of firelight reached up from the desert ravine.

He wondered what Curt looked like at that very moment, burnt to a crisp, skin seared from his flesh, bones blackened by the obliterating heat. He wondered what Curt smelled like, too, and whether it would whet his appetite.

Pete found himself laughing.

Okay, hoss...stop fucking around.

Gotta get back to that shitpile of a house and do the dance.

The stretch of desert where he and the others had taken the girl very much lived up to the word. It was *deserted* as shit, though he firmly believed that the law was onto the kidnapping already and it would only take time for them to ride out, this deep, into the Mojave wilds. The search would take place within the limits of Las Vegas, initially. At least for a day or so. For now, there was no one out here but himself, crispy deep-fried Curt, and all those bitches back at the old cobweb-infested shithouse.

Still...

Life had a way of pissing in Pete's cornflakes.

He'd always considered himself born under a bad sign, just a simple guy who could have - *would have* - made something great out of himself were it not for his terrible luck and the stupidity of others around him. Had he been gifted with the sort of luck that others enjoyed, there'd have been no jail time, no bullshit job at Curt's garage, no fat, useless bitch like Lisa clinging to his side and demanding money for a bratty, wimpy kid he'd never even wanted...

He'd have been free.

Free to do what he wanted, go where he wanted, *take* what he wanted. No matter what, or *who,* it was.

Pete spat another glob of blood and phlegm to the ground.

He thought of Jess.

He thought of all the long years he'd known Curt, how his *'friend'* had always ensured his dear wife was kept at arm's length. The bastard had never trusted him. Sure, he'd made excuses as to why Pete had never met the woman, but Pete had seen photos and on seeing her in real life when this whole damned train-wreck had kicked off, he'd known the real reason why...

Jess was a *ten.*

Shit man...she's an eleven.

She was a walking, talking fuck-toy; a sumptuous piece of meat just dying to be chewed up and spat out.

He grinned, forgetting the pain.

First, he'd kill his cunt ex-wife. He'd make it quick, get her out of the picture before he handled the rest. An obese, disgusting mess, the cunt may be, but she was *tough.* She had a right hand on her that could drop a fucking heavyweight and if that bitch got on top of a fella, he'd be dead before he heard his ribcage crack open like a piñata.

Yeah, he mused. *You first, Lisa...you first. You won't even see it coming, you fat fuck.*

And after I've dealt with your *repulsive ass...*

Then I'll get to know Jess a little better.

More than a little.

I've seen the way she looks at me, I know she wants what I got. And now with that do-gooding husband of hers cooked like a Christmas turkey, she'll get exactly *what she wants, needs and fucking* deserves.

Pete felt himself grow hard in his jeans as he picked up his pace, walking more purposefully now. He reached down and stroked his cock through the rough fabric. In his mind, he saw Jess, lain out with her legs spread wide, her pussy glistening with desire as she beckoned him closer with one curled finger, her eyes lit with a hungry fire, her nipples, hard and rigid, her lips moist, her breath short.

Oh yeah, we'll have some fucking fun with her.

Open her all *the way up.*

Then we'll deal with that creepy fucking kid…

15

Before Jess had the bedroom's door all the way open, the sounds, and the presence, were gone.

They seemed to disappear into thin air; one second there and in the splinter of a moment no more than a doubtful memory. There was no fading off into the distance, no echoing of the strange, somehow maleficent chittering that had accompanied the heavy thumps. The nightmarish shadow of the thing inside that had so terrified her had simply blinked from existence, dispelled by the flick of a light-switch.

The room was just a room.

Four walls, a roof, a faded carpet, old floorboards, a grimy window with a faded wisp of curtain.

And one sweet, smiling little girl.

Jess looked at the girl, confused, panic-stricken and more than a little frightened.

When she saw it, she almost screamed.

A shadow loomed over the small child.

It seemed to cling to Emily's aura like a translucent blanket, wreathing her in darkness, moving free from the laws of the natural world.

It seemed...alive.

Jess reeled, though the scream never came, for in the fraction of time it took for her to register the malignant vapor, it vanished, fading from existence like a shadow from the sun.

It was gone.

Just like the sounds.

Just like the shadows she swore she'd saw beneath the bedroom door. Gone.

Did I just see that? she fretted. *Did I see* any *of it? Did I really?* When no definite answer came, Jess instead locked her attention onto the girl.

Emily was sat atop the worn-down bed, staring intently at a comic book as though it was the only thing that mattered in all the world. She seemed completely unaware of the looming, evil murk that had clung to her only seconds ago.

That, or she just didn't care.

Jess' eyes scanned the room from top to bottom, searching every corner, resting momentarily on the window, still partially open and with a gentle draft wafting through it. Nothing was disturbed. Nothing was out of place. Besides the ruffling of the comic's page as Emily turned it to gaze lovingly on fresh new images, there was no sound at all.

Oh, dear sweet Jesus, what the hell is going on here...?

Jess wondered if perhaps she really *was* losing her mind.

No one would blame her if she had.

She'd been through a lot in the past few years – great pain, unthinkable loss, the crippling, life-altering illness. And now this terrible shame at having kidnapped Emily.

Could that be it? Could she have cracked and was currently spinning off into the fun-filled realm of evil hallucinations and perceptual distortions?

Sanity was malleable, after all.

But that explanation was bullshit and she knew it.

Insanity…the stress of the situation heralding the collapse of her reason…it was an easy answer, but she didn't buy it.

Her state of mind was just fine, thanks.

There'd been no slow build up to breaking point. Even with all that she and Curt had been through she'd never once felt the breath of madness whisper in the space between her ears. When tragedy struck, she'd survived it, when the illness came, she'd quietly accepted it.

She *had* gone along with Curt's desperate plan, *that* was pretty damned crazy, though she'd done it not for herself, but for *him*.

Jess had been ready to die.

She'd made her peace with it.

Oftentimes, while Curt was out at work, earning their next meal, she would grab a deckchair and drag it outside their trailer. She would place it outside facing West, sit down in it with a cold beer in her hand and watch the sun set over the Mojave plains. Like a water painting, the skies would change ever so subtly. If she watched them without pause it would be impossible to pinpoint the moment when orange bled into red and red gave birth to purple. It just happened. The change was such that perception was all but impossible. Jess thought of life that way; always in flux, always undergoing a beautiful transformation. She'd come to believe, in those quiet, reflective months, that life and death were much like the setting sun – no more than a shifting of the light as rebirth took place elsewhere.

In death, Jess would be at peace.

Peace with life, peace with pain, peace with disease and, in that final moment when death took her cooling hand in its own, she'd find peace in the sweet reunion she believed with all her heart would come to pass.

Curt, though...

What would become of *him*, left behind in a world where all he held dear had been stolen from him?

What would become of her husband?

He wouldn't have made it alone.

Jess knew it in her heart. As strong and able as he was, Curt was teetering on the edge of a *different* aby. One of dark, inescapable despair. Her death would have tipped him over the precipice's rim and down he would have fallen. Down and down and down, till the cruel, hard killing floor of his reality rushed up to meet him and shattered his essence to pieces.

So here she was, stood before a cute, intelligent girl whom she'd played a part in kidnapping, yet Jess herself felt like the little child lost.

She thought of the terrible shadows.

She still could feel the coldness that emanated from that terrible shadow.

That presence...

Looking down, she saw the tiny hairs on her arms had yet to recede. They sat atop a million raised pores as though scanning for danger.

She'd *seen* the shadows.

She'd *heard* the sounds.

And she *wasn't* insane.

And, back in the van, when she'd looked deep into the girl's eyes...

She'd seen something then, too, all the way back when this whole insane plan had begun.

Those things were real. All of them.

There was something wrong with Emily. Something that had nothing to do with being kidnapped, held in an old house, or abandoned by her family.

Then find out what it is, once and for all.

71

Jess moved closer to the bed. "Can I sit?" she asked quietly.

Emily's eyes never left her comic. Jess noticed she was now reading a *Spiderman* story. "Of course. I'd like that a lot. It's a little lonely up here."

Jess eased herself down onto the bed only inches from Emily. "You'll be going home soon, sweetheart. I…" Jess hesitated, "I promise."

The surety with which the girl spoke gave Jess chills… "No, I won't."

"Why do you keep saying that, darling?"

"Because it's true. I'll be in this room until I'm not."

What did *that* mean?

Jess quickly gave the dimly lit bedroom another search with her eyes. Nothing.

You saw it, the voice repeated inside.

It's now or never. Ask her.

"Emily?"

"Yes," the girl replied sweetly.

"Can I ask you something, please?"

"Sure," Emily said, non-committedly. Whereas before Jess had marveled at the girl's quiet self-confidence, even admired it, now she almost feared it. Watching Emily sat on the bed with her mind fixated on the story, Jess thought of devils and deceivers, monsters wearing the suits of humans.

Deep shame ran through her, making her stomach lurch.

Yet the fear, the sense of the uncanny, held firm.

It took all the strength she had left inside her to ask the question. She formed it carefully, unwilling and unable to dance around the matter any longer.

"Emily…" she said, ever so quietly. "Was something in here with you, just now?"

Without speaking, Emily slowly closed the comic book, being careful not to damage the pages, and laid it on the bed by her side. Finally, she looked up and met Jess' eyes.

When a smile slowly spread across the little girl's face, Jess felt like screaming.

"Yes," Emily said.

"What…what was it, Emily? What was in the room?"

"Do you really want to know?"

Did she?

"I do, Emily. I really want to know."

"Well if you really want to know, come closer..." Emily urged, speaking just above a whisper.

"I'll tell you my secret..."

Run, Jess. Run and never look back.

No! She's a child! Whatever this is that she's experiencing, she's still a child!

Jess leaned closer...

16

Curt's return to the world of the conscious was ushered in by unbelievable pain; a fanfare on re-entry that was purest torment. He groaned, spat a thick clot of sand and blood from between his lips and pulled his face from the desert earth as though peeling away a scab.

Where was he?

What the hell had happened?

It took a few seconds before the memories could push through the landscape of aches, pains, cuts and breakages that his body had become.

When they hit, they hit hard.

Pete!

The son of a bitch had left him to *burn*.

And, Curt recalled, he had plans for the girl, too.

I need to move. Need to get back to the house.

He's going to kill the girl.

Pete hadn't said it, not explicitly, but he'd implied it. And Curt had seen it in his eyes...that deep desperation that could drive a man to acts there was no coming back from. His workmate had all but left him for dead...tried to murder him to cover his own ass. There was no telling how far Pete would go to clean up this mess.

And it wasn't just the little girl who was in terrible danger. Jess was back at the house, too.

And his sister.

Terror bludgeoned Curt's senses.

How long had he been out?

Ten minutes?

Twenty?

An hour?

They could all be dead by now.

If Pete's laid a hand on any *of them...*

With herculean effort, Curt twisted his hips and rolled over. He lay on his back for a second, staring up at the night sky as he caught his breath. The stars above, cold and unconcerned, shimmered in the cosmos. The moon hung high.

Haven't been out long, he realized, studying the moon's position in the heavens.

Still too long, though. Still too long. Get up.

Taking a deep breath, Curt pulled himself up into a seated position using only the muscles in his stomach. He looked down upon himself, startled at the mess he was in. His shirt was soaked with blood from a hundred cuts and abrasions, his stomach, visible through a huge gash in the shirt, looked as though a wild animal had gone at it. The skin was split open in several places, scraped away to the wet meat below in others, blood flowed freely from the wounds, soaking into his groin. Below it his jeans were sliced to ribbons, revealing more wide and ragged wounds where sharp metal had cut through flesh. He wriggled his toes, breathing a sigh of relief when they all did their jobs correctly, bar one. In his left shoe, a toe - one of the smaller ones – screamed in protest as he wriggled. One down, nine intact. He could work with that.

Curt raised his left arm. At some point during his life-or-death scramble from the burning wreckage, he must have caught his fingers on something. Two of the nails on his left hand were torn off at the root. He studied the glistening, wet flesh beneath, wincing in pain as the night air kissed the tender open wounds where dirt and sand clung and burned. His index finger on the same hand was bent back at a terrible angle, too. It had swollen to almost twice its normal size and had turned a sickly black color. The fingernail, still intact, tickled the top of his hand as the mangled digit rested where it had no right to rest.

Could be worse, buddy.

Could be your *right* hand…

There was no chance of raising *that* for inspection.

The damage wrought to his lower right arm by the crash was severe. Curt dared not study the splintered bone, jagging from the pulped flesh like a rock from the red sea. Instead, he studied the hand on the end of that ruined limb. It looked *dead.* All coloration and life seemed to have been drained from it when his arm had shattered like a wishbone. He wondered briefly if he'd ever use the hand again.

If he survived at all.

You're in a bad way, sunshine. A bad goddam way…

Well, what was new?

Despite the pain, despite the fear, despite the world having kicked both he and Jess right in their collective balls for the hundredth time, Curt managed to laugh.

It felt as bitter as the blood on his tongue.

"Get up, Curt. Get. The. Fuck. Up…" he moaned.

Gritting his teeth against the pain, Curt laid his left hand in the desert sand. Immediately, the probing sand began pressing into the frayed, exposed flesh of his palm. It stung like a hundred wasps all angrily coalescing to attack a shared prey.

Handle it.

Jess is out there.

With him.

He pressed his palm down hard. With his left leg pulled toward him, he twisted his hips. There was a brief, terrifying moment when he believed his right leg might be broken…that perhaps he'd misdiagnosed the damage, imagined the movement and the feeling there and would now be fated to remain in the cold dirt like a lame mule till the scavengers arrived to pick his bones clean.

The blood in his veins found its passage and his right leg came to gradual, blessed life.

He was on his feet in under a minute fueled by dread, driven by love.

Then he was on the road back to the house, staggering through the moonlit desert like a card-carrying member of the living dead.

17

Where in the hell *are* those two?

With a grunt, Lisa pulled herself from her chair, pushing out the table with her gut as she stood. It slid forward, scraping the linoleum beneath the legs.

Ah, what the hell? she mused. *It's not like anyone will bill me for it.*

She made for the kettle, grabbed it, took it to the kitchen sink, filled it with fresh water, then she plugged it back into the wall socket, ever-thankful for the generator outback, even if she *had* been the one to think of it.

Not only that, but she'd been thoughtful enough to bring along all the home comforts, too. Her brother was a good man, but he had plenty enough on his mind, what with Jess' illness and all. And Jess…she was just about the sweetest darn girl in all the state, but if Curt was carrying a heavy load on his shoulders, then poor Jess was damn near being *crushed* by hers.

Pete…that worthless fuck…he couldn't organize a drinking binge in a brewery.

Sighing, Lisa watched the kettle boil. It wasn't much of a distraction from her deepening anxiety, but it was something.

In truth, she felt a little useless out here. The boys were doing their thing, Jess was upstairs with the girl doing her thing, but Lisa…well, there wasn't a whole lot else she could do now that it got down to it. But damn it, she could make a cup of coffee for that poor tired sister-in-law of hers. She could do that.

If her role was to be den-mother, then so be it. She'd do her job and do it well.

She cleaned out a mug while the kettle boiled, spooned in some coffee granules and added a little sugar. Not too much, just a small spoonful. No milk.

Just how Jess liked it.

With the kettle finally boiled, Lisa poured in the water, stirred and made for the stairs. She hollered up, slightly unnerved by the sound of her own voice echoing around the rickety old house. "Jess!? I'm coming up with coffee, darlin'. You want I should bring something for the girl, too?"

There was a moment's silence, then, from behind the door...

"I'll come down in a few minutes, Lisa, okay? I won't be long."

Lisa huffed. "Dammit, girl, it'll get cold."

"I'll be right there!"

Was that aggravation she detected in Jess' voice?

"You guys okay up there, darlin'."

"We're fine," Jess shouted back. "Just doing some talking."

"We're fiiiiine," the little girl shouted, sealing the deal.

Lisa smiled. "Well, I never," she said to herself. "Quite a kid, at that."

She turned around, shaking her head in amusement. It seemed the little girl was made with some true grit. She'd suspected as much, they all had.

It warmed Lisa's heart, soothed her some, to hear the ring of the young girl's voice. Boys were fine - her son, Billy, was a little angel fallen from heaven if ever there was a one - but girls...good girls...they had something magic.

She thought of Curt and Jess.

And what could have been.

Her mood quickly plummeted, her spirits sinking.

Damn it all to hell, Lisa, there ain't no point in fueling the fires of sadness. Things are hard-wrought enough without you wallowing in the past!

Lisa made her way back to the kitchen.

She was halfway down the long hall that led from the staircase to the kitchen, when she heard the kitchen's back-door opening. The blasted thing squealed like a stuck piglet, but *damn*, it was a welcome sound.

Picking up her pace, she raced down the hall, making for the kitchen, eager to see her brother, keen to hold him and hug him and thank the good Lord that he was okay.

No reason to worry after all, you daft old besom!

She hobbled down the hall, spilling coffee left and right...

...*Never you mind, you can make another cup*...

...and entered the kitchen, breathless and smiling.

Instead of Curt, Pete stood by the table.

He was grinning around the half-chewed sandwich that hung from his mouth. Lisa stopped in her tracks, searching the room for her brother.

"Happy to see me?" Pete asked, spitting pieces of bread from his lips. He had that look in his eyes. The same look he used to have when he'd properly tied one on – like the world was one big joke and he was the only smug son of a bitch in on it.

Why did drunk's always look so damned pleased with themselves?

Pete stepped around the table wearing that stupid look like he was wearing a bowtie to church.

"Where's Curt?" she asked, impatiently.

Pete moved in close. "Well…about that…"

"Well…?"

Pete headbutted her, square in the nose, shattering the bone beneath like it was little more than porcelain.

18

"Tell me your secret."

Emily opened her lips to speak, but said nothing.

"I want to understand. I want to help you, Emily."

Was that true, though?

Terror still lingered at what Jess had experienced from the other side of the door. The girl continued to give off an air of knowing calm that was deeply unsettling.

Still, the answer was yes, she did want to know. She'd go crazy, otherwise. She needed to understand. If what she'd seen and heard had been real then everything she'd been raised to understand was wrong, or at the very least, woefully naïve. If the supernatural – for she'd already decided that the uncanny was at work here – *was* real, then miracles could be real, too.

And Jess could sure use a miracle.

"I think I believe you." Emily said, finally responding. "But people always say that. They always say, '*I want to help*', but they never do. Not really. Even Mommy and Daddy used to say it, but really, they just wanted me to *change*. To be something I'm not. To be a normal girl."

Jess studied the girl's face, searching for a lie. There was none to be found.

"But you're not a normal girl, are you, Emily?"

Emily shook her head slowly. "No. I'm…different. Different from you, different from my mom and dad, different from *everybody*."

"Talk to me, Emily. Tell me what makes you so special."

"I don't quite know how to describe it. I can…" Emily paused, the words sticking in her throat.

"Go on…please."

"I can…*see things* inside people. Bad things…"

"Bad things?"

"Mostly, yes."

"Like a psychic?"

"I can see the inside of anyone I get close to. All the stuff they try to hide from everyone else. All the stuff that makes them ashamed or makes them afraid at night. I can see it all, even the things they can't see themselves…"

Jess let the words sink in, trying her best to process what the girl was telling her. She'd always thought of psychics as nothing more than charlatans, looking to make an easy buck from the gullible and the grieving.

In the last twenty minutes, that had all changed.

Seeing a small girl wreathed in a living shadow would do that to a person.

Which brought her to the real question. One which she feared to even ask.

"Emily, what was in the room with you, sweetheart, can you tell me?"

"In the room?"

"Emily…I heard it. I…I saw something just…fade away. I promise you, you can trust me."

"You don't want to know…"

Jess' skin crawled. "Why not?"

"You'd only get upset with me."

"I wouldn't, I promise."

Emily frowned. "That's what everyone says, too! You shouldn't make promises you don't know that you can keep!" she said sternly.

"I'm sorry, you're right, but I feel like I'm losing my mind. I need to know."

Emily seemed to think it over for a second, then she spoke.

"It was Pete's"

"Pete's?" Jess asked, confused. "Pete's *what?* What do you mean?"

"You know how I said I can see inside of people?"

"Yes."

The girl flushed red, looking embarrassed.

"What is it?"

"It sounds *silly*, saying it out loud."

"It's okay. I won't make fun of you. That's the *last* thing I'd do. I'm practically scared out of my mind, Emily. Please, just tell me."

 Emily took a deep breath.

"Well…I can do other things too, besides see inside of people."

"I'm listening."

"I can see where they're going…"

"Where they're going?"

"Yes…I can see where they're going when…"

"When…?" Jess urged. She was finding it hard to take in air.

Emily took a deep breath. Her startling green eyes seemed to darken as she struggled to word what she wanted to say.

"Do you believe that you have a soul, Jess?"

Jess, caught off-guard, said, "I…I don't know. I hope so. I mean, what's the point of all this if we just die and it's all over?"

"So, you believe?"

"I…I don't know."

"I don't mean like in a bible or any of those silly books they teach little children, but an…energy…like electricity, that lives inside us and changes form when we die?"

Jess thought about it. "I guess I do. Everything has to go back to the source, right?"

"Then do you believe there's a place, or places, where our minds, or our souls, go when we leave here? Do you believe in that?"

Jess had no time to answer. The girl was determined to say her piece. "My Mommy does. Daddy, too. They never used to believe. They used to say that there was only this life and then a whole lot of nothing. That we all turned to dust and ash and that it was okay, because we lived on through the ones we loved. They said there's nothing beyond what we see and taste and hear and feel, but there is. They know it, now. They've seen…they've seen where people go. At least a glimpse of it."

"I'm not sure I understand."

"Do you believe in a Hell, Jessica?" Emily asked bluntly.

"Hell? No. I mean…I don't think so, I…"

"Then you're *wrong*."

"I am?"

"We all have a bad place inside of us, Jess. And a good place, too," the girl said with growing confidence. As Emily spoke, Jess sensed in her the wisdom of one much, much older.

She was a child, yet she was more.

Much more.

"Good places and bad places are inside us all. We all call them different things, but I call them Heaven and Hell because I don't know any other words for them. Their doors are always open to us and none of us know which door we'll pass through, Jessica, though we're drawn, always, to both. We each have our own bad place. Most of us never ever go there, though it's always there waiting for us. Your Hell is different from my Hell, your Heaven different from mine. If you listen closely enough to your dreams and your nightmares at night you can hear both places calling to you."

Jess tried to fathom the girl's words. Her mind reeled with terrible possibility. "You said that thing in here with you...that it was 'Pete's'. What did you mean by that?"

"The thing that was in here...that was from the bad man...*Pete's*...bad place. I found it funny. It's never scared me." Emily frowned. "*He* won't find them funny, though. Not at all."

"Pete?"

"The things that live in his bad place are very impatient to get started on him. I can open the doors to that place, Jessica. I can open the doors and I can let the things inside *leak out*."

Jess wasn't sure how she felt about any of this. It was one thing to claim a psychic ability. It was something altogether different to claim that she could give form to the formless.

Open doorways.

Even show people their own Hells.

That was what Emily was claiming, wasn't it?

Jess envisioned the black shadow she thought she'd seen when she swung open the door. A many limbed thing, already breaking apart into an ethereal mist. It had been right above Emily and it had faded before her eyes, to nothing. So strange had the vision been, Jess had doubted her own sight.

She concentrated hard, trying to envision every single detail of the strange shadow. It had been fleeting. No more than a fragment of a second, but she'd seen...

What?

Something huge. Something impossible. Something made of shadow and darkness.

And she'd sensed a sentience there, too.

It had been real. Emily was telling the truth, at least in part. The giant, vaguely recognizable phantasm *had* shared the same space as she and

83

Emily. That part had been real. Something *had* been in the room with them. A manifestation of some sort.

But an emissary of Hell? Something from outside our dimension?

It couldn't be. It was ludicrous.

A ghost was one thing. Jess' mind could comprehend such a thing as a psychically manifested spirit, but other worlds overlapping our own, existing in the same moment, yet out of time, places that were *alive*...

It all seemed inconceivable, despite Emily's steadfast conviction that it was true.

"Do they know what you are, Emily...your parents, I mean?"

Emily seemed to look inwards. A sadness touched her eyes. "*No one* knows what I am, silly. Not even me."

"Yet they're scared of you, all the same."

Emily nodded slowly, looking no more threatening than a scolded child, caught with her hand in the cookie jar.

It should have looked cute.

Normally it would have.

"They got scared after the last nanny was taken," Emily said quietly.

Taken. The word chilled Jess to her core.

She studied the child's face. Emily, having explained these spiritual dimensions with the surety and weariness of a mystic, now seemed so normal, spoke so childlike. She looked scared and ashamed.

"I'd hoped she'd just disappear and they'd think she'd run off, but Mommy and Daddy saw it happen. Not all of it, but they saw the worst of it, just before she was taken."

There it was again. *Taken.*

Jess' mind filled with cackling demons, towering fires, endless chasms.

"Was she taken to the bad place, Emily?"

"She was a bad person, so she went to *her* bad place, that's all. She was the first I sent away on purpose, the first since I was a baby. I didn't know that when I open the doorways and the things come for the bad people, their bodies are left behind. They suffer here before they're taken to their bad place. When her nightmares came to take her, they left a big, big mess."

Emily's sincerity chilled Jess to the bone.

"How was she 'mean' to you?"

"At first, she'd whisper behind my back, talking on her phone, telling her friends that I was a freak and a weirdo. She called me a little…" Emily froze. "I can't say the word."

"Why?"

"It's a cuss word."

"Okay."

"I can say another word instead. She called me a little…poop."

Jess, despite her wonder, her fear, her awe, almost laughed.

"I'm not, am I?" Emily asked.

"A poop? No…no, you're not a poop, Emily."

"Thanks," Emily said, before going on. "Anyway, then she started getting mad at me for nothing. If I talked during a movie or if I needed the bathroom after I'd been put to bed, she'd pick on me. She hit me once or twice, too. It wasn't very sore, but you shouldn't hit little girls."

Jess almost hoped this…*bad place*…was as real as Emily believed it to be. "No, you shouldn't. That nanny was a real…poop."

"All I wanted was to have a friend. I never meant to annoy her or get in the way."

"She should have been honored to be your friend."

Emily flushed. "Thanks."

"And are *we* friends, Emily?"

"Huh?" The girl seemed caught off-guard.

"You and I…are we friends?"

Emily's demeanor shifted with all the speed and fluidity that only a child could summon. "You took me away from my Mommy and Daddy, Jessica. That wasn't very nice. And you *still* don't believe me."

"I'm trying to, Emily…I'm…"

"I'll make you believe! Look…!" the girl commanded.

Something changed in the room as Emily spat out the word.

The air seemed to grow thicker, the walls seemed to press inward like huge collapsing lungs. Jess swore she could *hear* the walls breathing.

Then, from beneath the bed, right by her feet, came a high-pitched, keening cry, somehow both ancient and infantile. It gurgled as a child would, though there was no innocence in the sound. Immediately it was joined by others. A whole cacophony of wailing, howling, tortured infants, screaming in diabolical symphony.

Looking down at her feet, Jess saw tiny fingers move amidst the shadows beneath the bed.

Soon, they moved into the light.

They were the hands of children, *hundreds* of them, all seeking the light from the darkness beneath - withered, rotting, swollen with decay, bloodless and crawling with feeding maggots.

"*Mommmmmy*," the dead things croaked, cold and cruel.

Please God, help me!

Jess felt warmth spread across her groin and trickle down her thighs as her bladder loosed. Still staring in horror at the moldering babies slowly emerging from the shadows by her feet, she pleaded. "Emily…make it stop! *Please!*"

Emily's eyes brimmed with tears.

"Should I send *you* to your bad place, Jessica?"

Mortal terror flooded Jess' senses as the nightmare advanced. She watched, frozen to the spot as the maggot-ridden infant's hands clawed with muddied fingernails at the carpet, cleaving bloody gashes in the fabric that swelled with crimson as though the rug itself was made of flesh.

Though she spoke softly, Jess could hear Emily over the endless, deafening wails of the dead children.

"I think you're probably nice," Emily said.

As sudden as the horror had begun, it faded.

The tiny malformed hands receded back into the shadows and the pained, soulless cries of the unspeakable infants faded from the world as would night-terrors, dispelled by the dawn. The carpet, covered seconds ago by deep red gashes, seemed to weave itself together till there was no sign of the horror she'd witnessed. The blood seeped into the fabric, leaving no stain.

There was nothing in the room besides Jess and Emily.

She slumped to her knees by the side of the bed, weeping with relief. She tried to thank the girl with the terrible gift for closing the door on her own horrors, but words were lost to her.

"You've been kind to me, Jess. You've been nice."

Jess looked up from her knees at the little girl. The child was a blur through her tears.

Emily was perched on the side of the bed, smiling warmly. Meeting the girl's startling green eyes felt like stumbling over an abyss into insanity.

How could this be?

How could *any* of this be?

Emily was just a little girl, in love with comic books and chocolate and cartoons and all the things in this world that made the place worth living in. She was innocent.

But she had terrible power.

Jess watched without speaking as Emily hopped from the bed, her feet landing where only moments ago those babies...

...*dead* babies...

...had clawed and scraped.

Jess felt sick. Her soul felt scraped bare. Yet in the same moment a great elation rose within her. Emily could summon 'Hell'. Did that mean she could also summon 'Heaven'?

Jess wondered if this was what the apostles felt, sat by the feet of their messiah.

She followed the girl as she skipped lightly to the window, in awe and in terror of what she now *knew* to be true.

What had she and Curt gotten themselves into, here?

When the girl spoke, Jess listened as intently as would a disciple, gripped by a fervent awe that bordered on hideous worship.

"I'm going to do something soon, Jessica. I don't want to do it, but I need to. You won't be hurt, I promise."

Jess said nothing.

Jess *believed*.

"I'm going to open up a doorway. And you're not going to like it..."

PART 2

Castles and Sand

19

Pete watched, amused, as Lisa spat the remains of three teeth out of her bloodied mouth like unwanted candy. One of the teeth landed silently on the table-top, the other two didn't make it quite as far. They clung to her swollen lip for a second, then, lubricated by blood and saliva, they slid down her chin and dropped onto her mountainous bosom. They held there like little mountain climbers scaling a pink, fleshy Everest.

Not bad for one headbutt.

Not bad at all.

He still had it.

The fat bitch looked like she was set to topple.

With one hand, he clutched her shoulder, balancing her. With the other, he grabbed a freshly opened beer from the table.

"That's it, bitch. Get 'em all out. Wouldn't want you choking to death on your own teeth, now would we?" Pete asked, cheerily. "Not yet, anyway."

Lisa said something, but he had no idea what. She sounded all kinds of fucked up.

"The girl's still upstairs, right?" he asked.

Lisa managed a small nod. Her head was rolling wildly on her neck, though. It looked like her melon might fall off any moment.

"And Jess is with the girl…?"

Another swaying, intoxicated nod.

"That's good. I'll get to those two bitches soon."

Lisa tried to say something else. More gibberish that he couldn't understand. He wasn't much interested anyhow.

Pete chugged on the fresh beer, relishing its taste after his brief but wholly fucked-up trek through Bumfuck-County, USA. Damn, it tasted good. The fat sow had her uses. Stocking up the little portable fridge she's brought along sure was one of them.

Shame Curt wasn't here to share in the glory of it.

Pious prick would probably shut me down for being 'drunk' during business.

Motherfucker.

Well that wouldn't be much of a problem going forward, now would it? There wasn't a bottle of beer on God's good Earth that could put out Curt's fire. No, sir.

Pete chuckled to himself, despite the headache. It had only intensified since he'd used his forehead to crack open the fat, disgusting food-disposal unit he'd once called 'wife'.

He lowered his beer and, still with a fistful of her hair, directed Lisa to a chair. She sat there, limp as a used-up dick, blood and snot spilling from her beautifully flattened nose onto her split, swollen lips.

Yep…a job well done.

Taking his time, Pete pulled up a chair by her side. He sat close, making sure he was her whole world, relishing the fear that brimmed in her eyes. It was nice to finally put paid to the cunt. He should have done it years ago when they were still together.

Regrets, I've had a few…

"So…" he said. "You're probably wondering just what the fuck is going on, huh, cunt? That's okay. Makes sense. It's not every day your ex-husband wanders in from the desert night and rearranges your face. It's a good look, though. It suits you. It ain't like I could make you any fucking uglier." "Now…" he said, scratching his stubble. "I have no idea what in the *hell* you just said to me, Lisa, but I'll hazard at a guess…

"You were asking where your kid-brother is, am I right?"

Lisa nodded. Tears streamed down her face in little rivers.

"Thought so. Well, to answer your question, Lisa, your brother and I had a bit of a disagreement. You see, when we got to the phone, we did as we'd planned…we called. Then we called. Then we called *again*…

"There was no answer. None. Zilch. Zip. Sweet *fuck all*. Now…considering where we are and who's kid we have upstairs, we needed a change of plan, and quick. See, it was looking like the money wasn't going to be coming our way, after all. Which means all *this* was for naught." Pete waved his arms to accentuate the scale of their efforts. "I figured we just cut and run, if you know what I mean? Keep it simple, just cut the kid's throat or somethin', then bail. We could all go back to our shitty little lives and maybe even get away with it. Me…I'd have made for Mexico. Fine looking bitches down there.

"But would Curt listen…? *Nope*. Captain do-gooder thought we should let the little lady go. Now, you guys are all nobodies, but I got a criminal record that's nearly as long as my dick, and should the little cunt upstairs identify me, I'd be picked up in approximately ten seconds by the feds. Not to mention - and I have to admit, I kept this to myself - my plan all along was to kill the kid. *You* fucking assholes just *had* to take the moral ground and have her comforted by Curt's bitch. She's seen *all* our faces, Lisa. Did you three dumb *fucks* really think I'd have let the kid walk once we got the cash? You're not so good at this whole 'crime' thing, are you?

"Anyway, none of that shit mattered one bit, not to him. Curt wouldn't allow the girl to come to any harm, under any circumstances. Typical of the prick, right?"

Lisa opened her mouth to say something and expelled only more blood. Her eyes drifted around the room drunkenly. Pete reached forward and patted her on the cheek.

"You still in there?" he asked. "So…I couldn't allow him to set the kid free, and we got into a bit of a tussle. At around sixty miles per hour, too. Curt ended up flipping the fucking van! Can you believe that!? It was a hell of a crash, Lisa. Not much of a driver, your brother…about as good a driver as he was a criminal. I was lucky as hell to get out of there with all my limbs still attached to my body."

He leaned in so close he could smell her blood, feel her hitched breaths tickle his stubble.

"Curt wasn't so lucky."

Lisa was sobbing now. She was still quiet, still half the world away, but the news of Curt had registered. Pete was surprised she hadn't tried to alert Jess in some way, but she was a smart gal. He figured she probably understood that to alert them would only serve to put them in his crosshairs all the sooner.

Either that, or he'd really knocked the sense out of her.

Didn't matter either way…he'd deal with the two upstairs soon enough.

He turned his attention back to the situation at hand.

"I'm sorry to have to be the one to deliver the news to you, Lisa, but baby brother is currently burned to death in a ditch, about two miles up the road. I think his death is terminal. Bad luck for Curt, huh?"

Suddenly Lisa was up from her chair and lunging for him.

She came at him like a feral grizzly.

Startled, Pete leaned back too far, his chair toppling and sending him spilling to the floor. Before he had a chance to think, Lisa was on her feet above him, and brandishing a kitchen knife.

Where the hell did she get that?

From the table, dipshit!

It didn't look sharp, but a knife was a knife and, given the right amount of murderous rage, a person was capable of anything.

And his ex-wife was just *bursting* with murderous rage.

She half moaned, half growled something, then she was raising the knife over her head. She swayed in place like a great tree, ready to fall.

Thinking fast, Pete raised his right leg, drew the knee back and then kicked forward.

There was a high-pitched whine as his boot connected with her stomach, followed by a shower of blood and spit that showered down on him like a red rainfall.

Disgusted, he dragged himself to his feet.

Lisa was leaning over the table now, fighting to catch her breath. The knife was still clutched in her hand, though it appeared to be all but forgotten.

How in the hell was she still standing?

The bitch had some fight in her.

Pete grabbed a handful of her hair and yanked her head around. For a second, he thought he might have broken her neck, but she moved into the motion until she was facing him.

Jesus, she was a mess.

Pete laid one on her, right beneath the left eye.

There was a muted grunt from Lisa, all the fight leaving her at long last. He let go of her hair. Lisa crumpled and hit the floor, dead to the world. He fancied he could feel the house shake when her massive bulk hit terra-firma. It was enough to justify a fucking earthquake warning.

Thank Christ she never fell on me.

I'd be flat as a Taiwanese whore by now.

Catching his breath, Pete stood over her. She was actually snoring.

How about that...? he laughed in surprise.

Had no idea that was even a thing!

Every day's a school day.

"Okay, Lisa. One more, for old time's sake, then we'll get this show started properly, whadd'ya say?"

Pete raised his right foot from the blood-slick floor and stomped his boot down on her face, like he was stomping a bug.

"Did you hear that?" Emily asked. "Downstairs…?"

Jess, hadn't heard a thing, lost as she was in the terrible reverie of what she'd witnessed take place with her own eyes. Everything she'd believed about the world was a lie. There was no logic to the universe. No pre-ordained pattern to the natural world. Everything she'd thought she understood, she now realized was a nonsense. A fiction. A safety net to protect the human mind against the darkness pressing in from all sides, just out of sight.

She was a child again, lost in a dark and dangerous world, where magic was real and could reach out and grab you from the shadows, tearing your mind and body to bloodied scraps.

A place where monsters, too, were real.

Since Emily's display of power, Jess had been rooted to the spot, still as stone, her mind spinning down endless corridors of dark possibility.

The girl could open doors in people's minds.

No…not in their minds.

In their *souls*.

Unimaginable as it was, Emily had the power to bridge worlds.

What else could she do? What had she *seen*?

Had the girl conversed with Gods? Had she stood before Devils? What would she be capable of as her powers began to grow with age, wisdom and experience?

Nothing was outside the realm of possibility anymore, not when babies…

…*dead babies*…

…could crawl from beneath a bed and scratch blood from a carpet like it was made of skin.

"Jess," Emily said, grabbing her by the arm. "You should go see what's happening down there, I think."

"Huh?" Jess asked, miles away, drifting on a sea of confusion and wonder. Again, Emily tugged at her arm. And suddenly, she was back in the room, pulled from her terrible awe and glad of it. "Shit…what's going on?"

"I think you should go see what's happening downstairs, Jess. It sounded like there was shouting." The little girl looked concerned and for a second Jess could almost believe she was a normal child. Just an everyday kid who liked comics and She-Ra and Mario Kart and...

She can send people's souls to...

Where?

Hell?

Don't think about it. Not now.

Jess gave herself a shake. "Emily...I..."

"I know. Please, don't be scared of me. I needed you to believe. And I meant what I said, I think I trust you. I don't want to hurt you."

"You *think* you trust me?"

"Can that be enough, for now?" Emily asked.

Did it even *matter* whether it was enough or not?

What Emily wanted, Emily would get.

Jess studied the girl's startling, emerald eyes.

She cast her mind back to when all this had started. In the back of the van. Staring into the endless depths of the girl's eyes. Seeing herself reflected there.

Screaming.

"You should go and see what's going on."

Jess still felt far away. "Yeah...yes...I'll go see. It's probably Curt getting back."

"You really love him, don't you?" Emily asked. "I can tell. I watch lots of movies. Some of the people in those movies look at each other the way you look at him. The boy on the Titanic looks at the girl that way. I never understood why she wouldn't share her floating wood with him."

Jess amazed herself by bursting into laughter. Despite all she now knew, Emily could still disarm her with innocent charm.

"I do...yes." Jess knelt before Emily, while the girl shifted around on her butt till she was comfortable on the bed. She was already picking up a comic book and set to lose herself in its pages as though nothing had happened.

Wondering if gods read comic books, Jess took Emily's small hand in her own.

"Emily?"

"Yes?"

"We took you from your home and I'm so, *so* sorry for it. I know Curt is, too. We were desperate. So desperate. And sometimes desperate people do desperate things. I'm telling you this because you say that you maybe *could* trust me. I want you to know that you can. You really can. And I'm asking you…no, I'm *begging* you, to trust me when I say that Curt is a good man. Do you understand what I'm saying?"

Please don't hurt him.

Please.

"Okay," Emily said, nodding.

"Okay?"

"Okay."

Was the girl being willfully obtuse? She had no idea. Emily was an enigma sealed within a great and secret puzzle.

She asked no more.

"I'll go see if they're back."

Emily looked up from her comic. "I think they are. I think I heard something smashing, too."

"Probably just my friend down there, breaking another coffee mug. She can be pretty clumsy at times."

"Probably…"

She thought about what the girl had said.

Open a doorway.

All the way.

And you're not going to like it.

"Emily…is there something you want to tell me?"

Emily, all innocence and light, replied, "No. Not a thing."

Jess made her way down the stairs slowly, moving as though through a quagmire. Stunned by what she'd seen and heard in the room behind, she felt as though she was passing through some secret door and into a world where nothing real held sway, where nightmares took form and fantasy could turn deadly in the time it took to blink. She worked her way downwards, stair by stair, moment by moment, only half-aware of where she was going and why.

What in the hell am I doing?

Something going on in the kitchen...

A crash.

No big deal. Lisa being Lisa...

Where was I going?

Or Curt. Maybe he's back.

I hope it's Curt. God, how I hope it's Curt!

I need to tell him. I need to make him see.

This whole thing…this kidnapping…it had to stop. He had to listen to her and if he didn't…

If he doesn't, she thought as her blood seemed to freeze in her veins, *Emily will* make *him listen and, dear sweet Jesus, don't let that happen, please.*

She moved from the bottom stair to the hallway and drifted down the long corridor towards the kitchen, wondering just how she would handle things if Curt thought her mad. Yes, he was a good man, a trustworthy man, but what she'd seen…

It was impossible. No sane person would take her word for it.

Jess needn't have worried.

All thoughts of how he'd react to cancelling the plan were wiped from her mind when she stepped into the kitchen.

"Lisa!?"

Her sister-in-law lay, spread out, on the kitchen floor, with her hair strewn around her head, soaked black with blood. Lisa's nose was pulverized, mashed into her face, flattened, ruined. Thick blood oozed from the mess like oil, running into her mouth, over lips torn to shreds. What remained of her teeth were peppered around her neck and chin, some stuck in the coagulating blood. Others, Jess saw, gathered between her ample bosoms.

Jess quickly scanned the room, searching in the shadows and peering down doorways for the assailant. Whomever had done this to her poor sister-in-law...they had to be close.

In Lisa's hand, a knife.

Jess fell to her knees before Lisa, immediately taking Lisa's wrist in her one free hand while she grabbed the blade with the other. Her eyes darted madly around the room as she searched for a pulse, expecting at any moment to be attacked by the bastard who'd done this.

"Please, Lisa...please be alive..."

Lisa's pulse was there, slow and dangerously weak, but it was there. Jess swallowed hard.

She lowered her face to Lisa's ruined mouth and felt the softness of the woman's breathing.

Good, that was good.

"Lisa! Wake up, honey! It's me...it's Jess."

There was a second or two of silence, then, instead of words, Lisa coughed out a mouthful of blood. It sprayed Jess in the face and she ignored it, relieved that her friend was coming around.

Lisa's eyes flickered open then closed. She blinked blood from her vision and peered up at Jess, confused.

"What the fuck?" she rasped. She sounded drunk, slurring badly as she fought to form words around the ruins of her mouth.

Jess whispered. "Lisa, honey, whoever did this is probably still in here. We need to get you up and get the *hell* out of here right now! Can you move?"

Lisa moaned something under her breath. The sound of her breathing – broken and rasping – filled Jess with fresh concern.

"Come on, babe. On your feet," she said, gently.

"Pete," Lisa gasped, fighting to breathe. "Pete."

"He's not back, Lisa. They're still out there. We have to go!"

"No! No...you don' understand...it was...it was him."

"What are you talking about?"

"*Pete did this.*"

Shock tore through Jess like lightning. "Shit..."

"Jess...run! Just get the girl and *go*. He'll kill you both. He'll..."

Lisa's words died on her lips. She stared over Jess' shoulder, her eyes wide and alight with fear. Her head shook from side to side. "No...No! You leave her alone you son of..."

Already knowing who stood behind her, Jess spun around.

Pete, painted in blood that was not his own, smiled down at her. "Surprise," he said to Jess.

Then he kicked her in the face.

22

Jess went down hard, grunting as her head collided with the kitchen floor. She clutched the knife in her left hand and prayed he hadn't noticed it before he'd attacked. To her side, she could make out Lisa, fighting to get to her feet. A swift kick from Pete to the big woman's ribs stole whatever fight she had left in her. Jess heard something cracking as Pete's boot landed the devastating blow. Lisa was wheezing, as though on her death bed, when Pete swung a second vicious kick at the big woman's temple. The crack was sickening. Then Lisa, again, was out cold.

The grinning maniac turned his attention to Jess.

She moved to get up.

"Now, now…" Pete admonished. He swung out again with his foot, aiming for Jess this time, catching her beneath the chin. Jess' head snapped back, blood sprayed from her mouth as she collapsed once more on the floor.

Pete stood above her, his feet on either side of her. He looked enormous, like a giant torn from terrible myth, looming over its next meal.

Jess spat at him. "Fuck you!"

"We'll get there, hot stuff," Pete crooned.

With all the strength she had left, Jess swung the blade upwards with her left hand, aiming for his crotch.

Her arm got no further than an inch off the floor, before Pete brought a punishing boot down on her hand.

There was another sickening crack. Jess screamed as her fingers snapped like wishbones under his heel. Someplace, off in the distance, she could hear metal hitting the floor as the knife slid uselessly from her destroyed hand.

"Won't be jacking off old Curt with *that* hand again, baby," Pete laughed. Turned her head left, Jess stared in horror at her hand. The fingers jutted out at crazy angles. One of her nails was torn off. The glistening skin beneath was bloody and ragged.

"Now," Pete said. "What was it you said? Oh yeah…. *'fuck you'*. I like the way you think, bitch. Your wish is my command…"

23

At the foot of the stairs, Emily listened.

She could hear everything that was going on down the hall and it hurt her heart.

She didn't want to see Jess in pain, nor hear it. She liked her. She hadn't lied when she'd said it.

She'd only half lied when she said she trusted her, too.

Jess had been part of all this. She'd brought her here and she'd put her in danger, or *thought* she had, but she seemed genuinely sad about it.

It had been hard on the girl, showing Jess the things she'd shown her. There was no pleasure in seeing the fear bristle and simmer in someone she liked.

But it had been necessary.

Just as it was necessary to allow the horrible man in the kitchen to do what he was doing, at least for a time.

In her short life, Emily had seen terrible things. She understood horror. She was acquainted with death. With pain.

Her parents had turned on her, just as she knew they would. They'd left her out here, surely hoping that the people who took her would hurt her bad. Kill her, even. They wanted her gone. They wanted her dead. She knew it, just as surely as she knew the man downstairs wanted the same thing. When the bad man realized her mom and dad weren't going to go along with the plan, he'd come for her and he'd hurt her. She read a lot of comic books. She watched a lot of movies.

These things always ended only one of two ways...

With smiles and love and relieved embraces, or with tears and heartbreak and bodies put beneath the ground before their time.

And there'd be no smiles at the end of *this* story, if the bad man had his way.

Emily winced as she heard Jess groaning in the next room. She knew what the man was doing to her. She'd seen *that* in movies, too. It was gross, but she understood that grown-ups liked doing it.

Or, at least, they liked doing it when they had a *choice*.

When it happened like it was happening now - to Jess - there was nothing good about it. It hurt the woman it happened to. It hurt her deep down in her heart, where hurt never healed.

Emily wanted to cry.

More than that, she wanted to go to Jess. To help her.

To make the bad man stop.

And she could. Oh, how she could.

She could make him scream and scream and scream, and it would last forever.

But she had to wait.

Jess had to *understand.*

The other man, the one Jess was with and who she said was nice…he hadn't come back. The bad man had probably killed him. Just as he'd kill Jess and the big woman and *her*, if he had the chance.

From the kitchen, she heard Jess plead. "No! Please…no!"

Then Jess screamed.

Emily covered her ears, feeling sick.

When the screaming stopped and the sobbing began, she wiped the tears from her eyes.

It has to be this way, she told herself. *Jess needs to know I can protect her.*

The bad man screamed himself then. Though there was no pain in it. No sorrow nor shame nor guilt. Only a delight and satisfaction Emily could barely understand.

And then, the kitchen fell silent.

Emily sat a moment longer, allowing the sadness to engulf her. She'd taken a great risk in allowing the bad man to do what he'd done. He could just as easily have killed Jess, then Emily would be no closer to her goal than ever. But that had been a chance she was willing to take.

Now, though, that the bad man had done what he'd wanted to do, Jess would soon be killed. Emily was sure of it.

She got to her feet and made her way down the hall.

24

"Damn, girl! That was fun!" Pete laughed.

Jess watched in mute disgust as he gripped his still-hard penis in his fist, squeezing until the last drop of his orgasm oozed from the tip of his cock and swung there like a little white tear.

Seeing her eying the thick, slowly elongating string of fluid, Pete feigned innocence. "Oh…sorry, baby. Do you want a taste? Is that it?"

Jess said nothing.

Laughing softly, he pinched the dangling pearl of cum between his fingers and pulled it free from his urethra. He licked his fingers clean. "Don't know what you're missing, bitch."

"Where's my husband?" Jess hissed.

Pete's eyes widened. "Oh shit! I'd forgotten about good ole Curt, what with fucking his wife in the asshole and all. Where in the good Lord's name are my *manners*!?"

Jess ignored his taunts.

"Where is he?"

"Have you any *idea* how long I've wanted to slip it to you, Jess? Have you any fucking idea? It's been a *long* damn time, let me tell you. Curt…he never even wanted us to meet," Pete flashed her a leering smile. "Guess he figured you'd fall for me or something, huh? Anyway, I saw you, baby. I saw you. Your asshole husband kept a picture of you in his wallet, wouldn't you know? Nice picture too. All folded up and all, but none of the creases were over your face or nothin'. He'd leave that wallet of his laying around all over the damn place. Fucking loser never had any damn money in it, so I guess he never felt none too protective of it? *Shit*, Jess…the times I had looking at your picture when he wasn't around. Used to spit my nut to it so hard you'd think I hadn't cleaned my tubes out in a month. Even got some of my milk on it once. Damn stuff shot so far outta my meat, it sprayed you right on the lips, Jess. Right on the fucking lips!

"Damn, if it wasn't fun! Still, though…there ain't nothing like the real thing. Getting you up here all alone like this, with Curt out of the way…it's all a man could wish for 'n' more. I'm sorry I had to nut in your asshole, but that's just the way it is. I prefer it that way. Nice and tight, yes, ma'am! Snug as a bug in a rug, up in there."

"WHERE IS HE!?" she screamed.

Pete pulled a frown. "Oh, shit, baby…sorry. Pardon my manners. I got myself a little carried away just then."

He loomed over her, grinning like the very Devil himself.

"Curt's dead, baby. He's with the angels now."

"You're lying," Jess cried.

She wished she could believe it.

"I'm afraid not, hot stuff. I'm afraid not. Now if you don't mind, I'm gonna have *you* clean your ass-juice from my cock. I want you to lick it good. And if you try to bite it, I'll cut your eyes out and use them on you like pleasure eggs."

As he spoke, his erection grew stiffer. Each word he uttered seemed to excite him more.

"I'll bite it off anyway, you piece of shit."

Pete looked momentarily disappointed. Then he smiled that dumb, self-satisfied smile. "Well then, in that case, let's just get down to the cutting, shall we, bitch…?"

He slipped an arm behind his back. When it came back into sight, he held a hunting knife. It shone in the soft light, its blade smooth and deadly.

From behind Pete, Jess heard a voice; soft and lilting, yet wreathed in anger.

"You're a very, *very* bad man…"

Pete had heard it too. He twisted his neck around, looking in the direction of the doorway.

"Well, if it isn't the little lady. Come to get a piece of me yourself, have you, rich kid?"

Jess realized she wasn't breathing. Amidst all the madness, all the horror, she'd had no time to think of the girl.

Now, though, Emily was the only thing on her mind.

Emily…and the promise the girl had made.

To open doors. To do what she had to do.

For Jess, time froze.

Pete grinned at the girl. "I had to take Jess in the ass, kid…I like the tightness, you see. But *you*…hell, you're young enough for the other hole. Why don't you come over here and say hi to Uncle Pete…?"

"I'm not afraid of you," Emily said. She wore a frown, deep and furrowed.

"And nor should you be, darlin'. I'll look after you good."

Jess met the little girl's eyes. Saw the hurt there. And was that shame she saw there too?

"I know what *you're* afraid of, though," Emily said softly, tearing her eyes from Jess and affording Pete her full attention.

Jess swallowed hard, remembering the horror Emily had shown her upstairs in the bedroom; a nightmare ripped straight from the deepest recesses of her very soul.

"And what's *that*, pretty girl?"

Emily shrugged her shoulders.

"You're afraid of spiders."

"Spiders?"

Her emerald eyes, brimming with warmth only seconds ago, filled with a stark, barren coldness, endless and cruel.

"Yes…" A smile touched the tight, angry snarl on Emily's lips.

"Big. Fat. Spiders…"

25

Pete took two purposeful steps towards the girl, towering over her. Emily stood her ground, her face flushed with fury. Jess watched from the floor, lost in a world of hurt and dark anticipation. Her face burned from her wounds, her stomach cramped tightly. In other more intimate places, the hurt ran deeper. A hurt she understood would never heal.

"Don't you hurt her!" she roared at Pete.

She tried to get up and found she hadn't the strength.

Pete laughed. "Hurt her? I'll do a lot more than *hurt* her, bitch." He spoke to Jess, though all his attention was fixed on the small girl stood in the doorway. Defiance and fury burned in Emily's eyes.

Jess twisted her head to the side and looked at Lisa. The big woman was still out cold. Jesus, the damage he'd done to her. Her face was a bloody ruin. Jess prayed she was still alive.

And what of Curt?

There was no time to even consider the things Pete had said, and had there been, they were too terrible to imagine.

With an agonized grunt she fought to sit up straight, reaching with her one good hand for the table leg, hoping to hoist herself up. She'd do what she could. She'd fight for the girl till she had no fight left.

Sooner be dead than have him hurt little Emily. Than have him…

She'd wrapped her trembling fingers around the wooden leg, blood causing the wood to slide from her grip.

Then she heard the sound.

Pete heard it, too.

He stopped in his tracks.

His head cocked to the side, listening.

Emily, Jess saw, wore a full, bright smile.

Yet in the child's smile, she saw a malice that distorted the girl's natural beauty, marring her innocence.

"What the fuck is that noise?" Pete asked, still emboldened but curious. He seemed more agitated than shaken.

Jess froze. All the air seemed to be sucked out of the room. Unreality washed over her as Pete's head swung left and right. He was trying to make sense of what he was hearing.

It sounded like heavy rainfall.

The tiny pitter patter of a thousand million tiny drops of rain. It was coming from all sides. They were on the bottom floor of a two-story house, yet it sounded like it was raining directly above her head.

In the room above, and even against the very walls.

Impossible.

Even from beneath her in the basement, the sound rose, as though it were somehow raining *upward* from down there.

No…

Not rain.

Something else.

Jess' heart seized, her mind reeled, as she realized what was making the terrible, unnatural sound. Every hair on her body stood on end as she listened, heard, *felt* the cause of the all-encompassing sound, moving behind the walls, the ceiling, on the lower side of the floor, beneath where she lay, crumpled and bleeding.

Oh, dear god…

Pete's wicked grin was gone. His face pallid, bled of color. He looked close to fainting as he began to realize that what he was hearing was not rain, nor was it anything natural.

"What the fuck are you doing!?" he demanded of the girl.

Emily said nothing. She met his increasingly frantic stare with a cruel smirk.

"What is this!?"

Jess knew.

In the name of all things unholy, Jess *knew*…

The sound grew in volume until it seemed to bore into her soul.

She followed Pete's line of sight as his head snapped to the kitchen window. Beyond the window, there was no desert night. Beyond the window, there was nothing.

The window was covered, every millimeter, every tiny area of glass, from top to bottom…

…with spiders.

They scuttled madly across the glass, seeking purchase, determinedly searching for a way inside the house. They were all sizes; some as small as a fingernail, some fat and swollen, as large as the palm of her hand.

A primal dread seared away her reason as she watched them madly crawl across and over each other, a thousand of them on the glass alone, a *hundred* thousand. She sensed their baleful eyes, black as night, soulless, abominable...

Ravenous.

When she heard the scream, it took Jess a second to realize the sound hadn't come from her own throat.

It came from Pete.

He stood in the center of the kitchen, spinning wildly, his eyes darting from ceiling to floor, then back to the window again. Always back to the window, where the hungry horde of arachnids scurried and crawled, separated from him by nothing more than fragile glass.

Jess struggled to rise, managing only to position herself upright. From her left, a new sound, still like rainfall, though now as though the heavens had vented their fury on a roof of metal or tin.

It was coming from the sink.

Wide-eyed and barely comprehending, Jess allowed herself to look. Though she couldn't see the plughole from her position of the floor, she could see the taps up there.

The taps, old and worn, rusted around the edges, were pouring what looked like a thick black liquid into the sink, and the sink was rapidly filling up.

The black substance had legs.

It had eyes, it had limbs, all fighting for purchase as the spiders poured from the taps into the basin. In seconds, the sink was overflowing. The spiders crawled from the sink's metal confines and made their way to the kitchen floor, some crawling down the woodwork, some slowly descending on webs. Others, larger ones, fell from the sink and landed by her side, where they quickly righted themselves.

Behind her, the rear door to the old house swung open with a slow, dreadful groan.

Rooted to the floor by his own stark terror, Pete let out a choked scream. His head shook from side to side, his mind unable to grasp what he was witnessing as, from the open door, a million more eight-legged, black and bristling nightmares scurried into the kitchen, their bodies shivering with anticipation. They moved as one, quickly navigating the kitchen floor till they covered all corners. Jess shivered as the bristling, living tide scurried around her sides, avoiding her, but close enough that she could see the light glint in their cold, dead eyes. With horrified wonder, she marveled at the spiders' terrible grace as they flowed like a stream, deftly scuttling around her hands, bypassing her legs and always, *always* with their cruel intent fixed on the panting, near-hysterical Pete. He was saying something to himself under his breath, over and over and over again.

Jess wondered if he was praying.

It wouldn't do him any good.

Looking up from the disgusting carpet of legs, eyes and fangs, Jess saw that the hallway to Pete's rear held the same horrors. A million more spiders covered every inch of the hallway's walls, floor and ceiling, forming a living tunnel. As she watched, a faded painting fell from the hallway wall, forced from its peg by the thick, broiling mass of arachnids. It fell to what had been the floor silently, the crash of its fall muted by the climbing, scurrying, agitated layer of spiders beneath.

There was no way out.

Pete knew it, too.

Behind him, Emily stood by the door, her face etched with a cold fury. As they had with Jess and, she noticed, with Lisa, the crawling mass moved around her feet, ignoring her completely. The girl stood there like a general amassing her armies. Within ten seconds more, the river of spiders had filled the entire floor.

Having covered the linoleum, they moved as one, crawling up the kitchen walls, climbing the table legs and covering its mass, spreading out like deadly shadow till the walls and table, too, were deepest, living black. The old grandfather clock that stood just within the threshold of the room disappeared as the spiders swallowed it in their relentless tide. The roof was next. Before she could properly digest the sheer horror of it all, Jess found herself utterly surrounded by the arachnids. She half-lay, half-sat on the floor with Lisa by her side, both untouched, both human islands in a hungry sea.

The spiders moved onward, towards their prey.

Pete had backed up into a corner of the room, his mind clearly unravelling as his phobia gripped him in its terrible power. On the walls to his rear, the spiders shifted in agitation. On the floor, they stopped just before his feet.

As sudden as it had begun, the terrible sound of the roiling spider army ceased. The room descended into a terrible silence. Jess blinked blood, sweat and dizzying terror from her eyes, watching as Emily's army - from the smallest spider to the largest – settled into a terrifying stillness.

Nothing moved.

The room held its breath.

Pete was whimpering.

"What is this!?" he shrieked, his eyes flitting from wall to wall, floor to ceiling. "Make it stop, cunt!" he begged more than demanded.

Emily turned her head towards him.

As one, the legion of spiders turned towards the petrified man in the corner, shuffling on a million bristling legs.

Countless cold, shining eyes fell on Pete, silently appraising their meal as he babbled madly to himself.

Jess, shocked into silence, shuddered in revulsion as the endless sea of eager horrors studied him.

"You shouldn't hurt people," Emily whispered, breaking the deafening silence that clung to the house.

"Please…" Pete whined through hitched breaths.

"You made my friend *hurt*. You'd make *me* hurt if you could, too…"

"Make it stop…please…I'll leave…! I'll go…!"

"You *will* go," Emily agreed. "You'll go soon. And you won't like it when you get there…"

"What are you!?" he half-growled, half-cried.

Emily cocked her head to the side, appraising the terrified, pathetic rapist, walled in by his own nightmare.

"Does it matter?"

Pete tensed. Jess could sense the bastard willing himself to flee. Fear gripped him like a fever, but instinct would soon override it.

He'd flee.

He'd *try*.

Emily met Jess' eyes, momentarily. In them, Jess saw concern. "Are you okay?"

Jess nodded slowly, too terrified to make a sound or move a muscle, fearing that the stone-still legion of spiders would turn their attention from the miserable bastard in the far corner and onto Lisa or herself.

That wouldn't happen, though, deep down she understood it.

This nightmare was all *Pete's*.

Impossible as it was, they'd sprung from the seeds of his darkest terror like wraiths.

And they'd come for he and he alone.

Jess knew it.

And Pete knew it.

With black fascination, Jess waited, her heart hammering in her chest.

"You'd better start running..." Emily said sweetly.

As one, the living ocean of fanged horrors bristled with purpose.

Then they made for Pete.

26

The moment the uncanny stillness was broken. The black wave of spiders pressed towards him as Pete's paralysis finally broke. Terrified, he ran blindly, with no idea of where he was going. The room, the *house,* was a living, writhing thing, eager to feed. He could no longer tell where the kitchen door was. It could have led him outside of this hellish place, but it had vanished, buried behind the trembling horde. It was simply gone, obliterated by an inches-thick swamp of the vile arachnids. That left only one option, one exit…

The hallway. Then, from there, the front door, wherever the hell *that* was.

Pete made for the open doorway, frantically brushing spiders from his hair as they descended on silken webs from the ceiling, pouring over his face, tangling in his hair, exploring every available orifice, seeking a way inside. He brushed them from his nostrils as they pushed and probed and dug.

Was he still screaming? He couldn't be sure.

He moved fast and was soon passing by the child…

…*monster*…

…who stood, untouched, still as stone amidst the black sea. He stumbled madly down the living hallway, feeling her vengeful gaze upon him as he lunged towards the living, crawling hallway. With each step, sickening crunches filled his ears, as dozens…hundreds…of the spiders flattened and burst beneath his boots, spewing internal organs from bulbous, swollen bodies.

He wailed as he slipped by the doorway, almost going down, only managing to save himself by grabbing the doorframe. More repulsive popping, crunching sounds rang in his ears as the spiders covering the doorway broke apart beneath his fingers, oozing thick, purplish fluid between his fingertips. The dead were quickly replaced, as those surrounding their obliterated family immediately began scuttling over his hand and arm. In seconds, Pete was wearing a sleeve of arachnids.

They began to bite.

With a shriek that only seemed to energize the spiders, he smashed his other hand down on his arm, squashing scores of the vicious little monsters into his skin. He pushed himself clumsily from the wall and desperately tried to brush off the surviving spiders. Where he cleared them, he could see the mass of tiny red puncture marks where the hideous creatures had sunk their fangs into him.

He'd been lucky.

The spiders that had found purchase on his skin had all been small. No larger than a house-spider.

Had they been the larger ones...

He had to keep moving.

To stop would be the end of him.

Pete moved down the writhing, breathing hallway, crushing the hungry fiends as he ran their hellish gauntlet, praying to God for an exit. When he made it through the churning, black corridor, he found no relief.

Instead, Pete's horror only intensified.

The single doorway leading to the living area was shut. Crawling over it were thousands more spiders.

And these ones were huge.

He'd seen videos of horrible arachnids that haunted the desert sands of Iraq, terrorizing the troops over there. They were enormous, abominations against all that was good in the world. The spiders scuttling across the wooden door looked even larger.

They moved with a terrible grace and will, their fangs visibly dripping with a clear fluid that could only be venom.

There was no way through.

Yet staying still was not an option.

On seeing the doors dreadful wards, he'd paused in his flight for only a second, and already the spiders that claimed the floor beneath his feet were scuttling up his boots, covering his ankles, scaling his jeans. Pete could feel them beneath the fabric, exploring the tender flesh of his legs.

Insane with panic, he smashed his fists into his jeans, mindless of the pain as he pummeled his own thighs, crushing the spiders as they dug and bit and fed.

One of the huge spiders on the door leapt from the throng.

Pete shrieked as the massive predator hurtled toward his face with the underside of its black, mottled belly exposed and its long limbs spread out like welcoming hands.

Screaming, he batted it from the air, horrified by the contact. It landed amidst the moving, black carpet, only a foot from where he stood. Then, at an alarming speed, it rushed towards him, moving atop the smaller spiders, crushing its brothers and sisters beneath its terrible weight.

With no sense of where he was going, Pete hurtled himself to the left, skidding on the sticky mulch beneath his boots.

He sped the only way that was left to him, though he was moving deeper into the nightmare with each step.

What choice did he have?

Black panic propelled him forward.

He grabbed the bannister, crushing more of the hideous spiders underhand, and flung himself up the staircase, half-crawling.

Behind, the horde followed, silently closing in on their prey.

27

As Jess watched, the sea of spiders slowly dispersed.

Those that hadn't given chase to Pete as he'd fled the kitchen had all but lost interest in their cruel game. Slowly and surely, as though working with one inconceivable mind, the loathsome horde made their way for the shadows permeating the corners of the dimly lit kitchen. They seemed to crawl *into* the darkness there, become a part of it, one by one, merging with the shadows until they were as insubstantial as the darkness itself, swallowed by it, embraced by it.

Jess wondered where the devils of one's nightmares existed, once the dreamer awoke.

Slowly, the creatures, seemingly borne of Emily's own will, became one with the shadow. Soon it was as though the whole terrible ordeal had been nothing but a vivid hallucination; the very definition of a 'bad trip'. The spiders had been physical entities, horrifyingly tangible, yet they evaporated like mist as though no more than phantoms. She studied the flow of arachnids with wonder and awe as they fled from a reality that, until very recently, Jess had considered concrete, slave to the laws of natural order.

When it came to Emily there *was* no natural order.

Wincing in pain, Jess used her good hand to hoist herself up. She leaned over the table for support, hardly believing that moments before, the table had been all but invisible. Buried beneath the terrible manifestations of Pete's inner fear.

As for Pete, he was gone now…chased by the remaining horde, to what end she didn't wish to know, lest it drive her to madness. She could still hear his screams, though they sounded so very far away, a distant wind whispering terrible truths from another world.

Across the room, Emily now sat on a kitchen chair, watching as the last of Pete's nightmares crossed over into the darkness of their own realm. She looked pallid, tired, worn down by the burden of her 'gift'.

Jess turned to her sister-in-law. Sometime during the insanity, Lisa had come around.

"Lisa." Jess knelt over her, gently taking the woman's badly shaking hand in her own. Lisa was a mess, but she was alive. Thank God, she was *alive*. Jess wondered what she, herself, must look like. Pete had done a number on them both. There was no question in her mind that he would have killed them if he'd had the chance.

If it weren't for Emily.

And her dark power.

"Am I dreaming?" Lisa asked.

"No."

"I'd better be, Jess," she pronounced it, *Jesh*. "Because what I saw…"

Jess nodded gravely. "I know."

"That was *real*, wasn't it?" Lisa asked, her voice tinged with terrible awe.

"It was real."

"They were *real*." Lisa gasped, her eyes wide with fright.

"They were…but it's okay now. They took care of Pete, Lisa. The spiders chased him away. We're safe."

"The spiders…" The words spilled from Lisa's lips like liquid dread.

"Try not to think about it. Just take your time, okay? Can you stand?" With Jess' help, Lisa struggled to her feet. She looked frail. More than that, she looked petrified.

"Easier said than done. Christ almighty, Jess…" said Lisa, momentarily forgetting the horror she'd witnessed. "What did he *do* to you?"

"It doesn't matter. It's over."

"Where is he? I must have blacked out during…"

"He's upstairs, or…"

"Or…what?"

"Or he's somewhere else."

"What do you mean, 'somewhere else'?"

Shaking her head, Jess said. "All that matters, is that we're safe now. All of us."

Realization dawned on Lisa's face. "Oh god, Jess…Curt! The bastard told me he killed Curt!"

"I know…I…he told me the same thing." Jess allowed the tears to come. Now that the madness seemed to be over, the thought of what she may have lost washed over her like a tsunami.

"Jess," Lisa mumbled around split and swollen lips. She still addressed her sister, but all her attention was on the small girl, sat on the

117

chair with her legs swinging back and forth. "What I just saw. What she just *did*...you have to tell me everything."

"I wouldn't even know where to begin."

From upstairs, there came the sound of a door crashing shut. The clarity of the sound stood in stark contrast to the man's distant screams of terror. He sounded far off, his voice traveling down a dark canyon, echoing off ancient walls. Jess thought of worlds colliding, merging, fusing as one.

"He's still up there! He got away! I'm going to kill the son of a bitch," Lisa snarled.

Jess was amazed and impressed by the big woman's resilience. She'd just came face to face with her own death, *and* something outside the natural order, and though she seemed to have missed much of what had occurred, she'd seen enough to send most people screaming straight to the mental hospital. The thought of her brother, dead at her ex-husband's hands, had shaken her from her fear at least for now. Breathing heavily, Lisa rose on heavy legs and took two stumbling steps to where Jess' knife lay on the linoleum. She bent forward, wheezing as she reached for the blade. "Fucking *kill* him..." she said to herself, spitting blood from threshed lips.

"You don't need to do anything," Emily said quietly, from her place on the chair.

Lisa, registering the girl's presence, looked confused.

Jess laid a hand on her shoulder.

Emily looked up at the ceiling, seeing beyond it.

"He's already dead..."

28

Pete moved along the upper hall, lost in a blind terror.

He was aware he was gibbering to himself as he stumbled from wall to wall, fighting off the hungry arachnids in a crazed, spasmodic dance. They flowed up the stairs to his rear, they swung on black silken webs from the ceiling, they coated the walls to his sides. He howled as a fat, black and purple spider, the size of his palm, dropped from above, landed on his face and made for his open mouth. His scream was suffocated by the abomination as it climbed inside.

Pete bit down hard.

There was a warm gushing sensation as his teeth ground through the vile meat of the spider's bulbous body, followed by a bitter taste that reminded him of uncut amphetamine. Pete gagged, spitting the halved spider from his mouth. Two of its legs, broken and mangled, he swallowed in his fright.

Behind him, the spider army rushed forward.

Pete looked up the length of the hall. He'd taken a turn somewhere and now had no idea where he was going.

Anywhere was better than where he was.

If he could find a room free of the spiders…If he could find a window…

Down the hall, he could make out the shapes of two doors, one on either side of the shadowy corridor. The light from his rear barely illuminated the gloom ahead, but it was enough to reveal that one door was writhing with the infernal monsters, and the other…

The other looked almost *clean.*

There were twenty or so small spiders scuttling across the length of the wood, no more than that.

Near-crying with relief and with a desperate hope kindling in his heart, he made for the door, his every footfall accompanied by the bursting, popping sounds of spider's annihilated bodies.

He was at the door in seconds.

He grabbed the handle and turned.

The door swung inwards. Pete rushed into the room, slamming it shut behind him.

Pete turned from the door.

There was a window.

And this one, like the door, was clear of spiders.

To Pete, it looked just like salvation. Moonlight shone into the room in a solid translucent beam, its radiant light, pure and welcoming.

Pete, teetering dangerously on the precipice of madness, giggled with delight. The room, dark though it was, looked entirely free of the hungry arachnids.

He was going to make it.

Pete moved toward the window, crossing into the soft light of the moon. He was half a meter from the blessed escape route when, from up and to the right of the room, he heard something move.

Pete looked up, into the shadowy corner above.

It took a second for his eyes to adjust to the darkness up there, where the light of the moon could not reach.

And when he saw what awaited him, poised, limbs coiled, nestled in its dark, impossibly huge web, he wished he'd been born blind.

The massive spider, easily the size of a large dog, opened its long, hideous limbs, uncurling them from their place beneath its black, mottled body.

Silently, it began to crawl from its web.

It moved with terrifying speed and grace, scurrying down the wall from its dark nestling place, its long legs reaching the floor in the blink of an eye. First two, then four, then eight. Its fangs jutted from beneath soulless eyes, slick with fluid.

There was no time to scream.

For Pete, there was only time enough to whisper the good lord's name. And wonder where his soul would lie.

Is sped towards him in a frenzied dash.

Then the spider was on him.

It curled its many legs around his shivering body, embracing him in an infernal grip, its black and bulbous head only inches from his exposed face. The eight purple orbs shone with feverish malice as it surveyed its meal. In the cruel mirrors of its eyes, eight terrified reflections stared back at Pete, gibbering, already insane.

And lower, below the pitiless eyes, its fangs.

There was no fight left in him. All his will had been crushed by the mere sight of the nightmare scurrying from its web. Pete could only watch, sobbing, as the huge incisors drew ever closer to his eyes until he could see nothing else in all the world besides the sharp points of the hideous mandibles.

He'd wished to be blind.

He got his wish.

The spider's fangs punctured both Pete's eyes simultaneously.

His world became darkness and pain. A terrible suckling filled his ears as the hellish arachnid fed on his juices while he bucked and writhed in its deadly embrace.

Despite the pain, Pete was glad for the darkness.

He was dead by the time the spider had shredded and eaten the better part of his face, and he hadn't seen one moment of it.

Wishes did come true.

Pete faded into forever on a sea of darkness, terror and pain, grateful for the end of all things.

His gratitude was short-lived.

He re-awoke in a place outside the world.

His body was whole once more, naked as the day he was born, renewed down to the last hair on his head. He could feel the musculature beneath his skin, the reality of his form.

Though he found out quickly that he couldn't move.

He was trapped, held in place, suspended above an abyssal darkness by thick, sticky ropes. A dim, sickly bluish light, its source unknown, illuminated the strange, alien realm.

It took a moment to realize he was using his eyes again.

And with his sight, Pete found himself introduced to his 'bad place'.

The web, vast and glistening, stretched on endlessly into the deep dark void.

All around him, in a wide circle and sat deathly still, spiders perched on its infinite strands. Some great, some small. Their numbers were endless.

There was a moment, a splinter of a second, in which the stillness held.

Pete felt the web shiver as a million arachnids anticipated their kill.

The silence was broken.

As one, they crawled.

The small ones filled his mouth, scuttling down his throat and silencing his pitiful scream.

The larger ones went to work on his renewed form.

Hungry fangs punctured Pete's ethereal flesh in a million places, feasting both inside and out, devouring the tender skin and the pulp beneath while he hung helpless in the endless web. Spasming in agony, choking on his own blood and the bodies of the feeding spiders piercing his gullet, Pete silently begged for forgiveness.

From God, from the Devil, from those he'd hurt, from all the cold, infinite universes his existence had affronted.

Forgiveness never came.

And the spiders fed forever.

"I have to go look for Curt," said Jess. "He might still be alive. For all we know he could be lying in a ditch someplace, bleeding to death."

Jess fixed her gaze on Lisa.

Christ, the woman was strong.

She was also damn near unrecognizable, her face a black and bruised tapestry of cuts and broken bone. When she breathed, a high-pitched wheeze came from her mashed, pulverized nose. Thick hardened blood, black as oil, clung to her nostrils and her teeth…

What teeth? Jess asked herself, dismayed.

She's lucky to be alive, never mind standing upright.

And so am I.

So am I…

"Lisa, honey…I need you to stay here with Emily. Can you do that for me?"

She'd never seen the big woman so scared.

The shock was wearing off now and despite her imposing bulk, Lisa looked as fragile and timid as a lost child. "With *her*?" she asked quietly, eyeing the little girl in the corner. Emily continued to swing her legs beneath her, lost in her imagination. Serene as a spring rain.

"She did what she had to do, Lisa. Just believe me when I say that she won't hurt you."

Lisa looked dubious. Jess could hardly blame her.

Lisa eyed the girl as though she was the devil, sprung up from Hell.

Jess wondered if perhaps the little girl was exactly that.

She turned her thoughts to where she needed them to be.

Curt.

He was out there, somewhere along the road. One way or another she planned to find him.

She took the big woman's arm gently and led her towards the quiet, bored looking girl on the chair. Lisa allowed herself to be directed, lost in a dark reverie, until she was stood before Emily. The girl turned her head up.

"He deserved it," she said.

Jess watched Lisa's reaction. She half expected her sister-in-law to turn tail and run screaming into the desert. And who would blame her?

Lisa cleared her throat. Jess winced as a fragment of broken tooth slid from her sister-in-law's shredded lower lip. "I know he did, honey," rasped Lisa.

Jess breathed a sigh of relief.

Lisa looked afraid, confused. Yet cutting through her dread of the girl, Jess could still sense the motherly instinct in the woman that she'd so long admired.

The girl would be safe with Lisa.

If she'd ever even *been* in any danger.

Jess pictured the river of spiders, the sheer, mind-cracking terror it inspired in Pete, his greatest nightmare brought to vivid, terrible life. She shuddered.

No, the girl had never been in any danger.

Not when they abducted her, not when she'd been confined in the room upstairs and certainly not when that sick son of a bitch, Pete, had set his sights on her.

She could have broken the man and destroyed him any time she chose.

The thought gave Jess pause.

Why had she waited so long to intervene? How long had Emily stood by, watching while he was raping her? How long before she'd chosen to come to Jess' aid?

She cast the thoughts out.

Curt was out there. Maybe still breathing.

Jess reached forward and touched the little girl's face. "Are you okay?"

"I'm fine. I hope you find him. I hope you can bring him back...your friend, I mean."

Jess smiled. "I hope so too, Emily. Lisa...?"

"Huh?" Lisa mumbled.

"You okay here?"

Lisa nodded resolutely. "I got this."

Her fear betrayed her stoicism.

"You sure?"

Emily piped in. "I'll look after her. We'll look after each other."

"Thank you, kiddo," Jess answered.

"Won't we?" Emily said, facing Lisa.

The big woman nodded again. "You bet your ass we will."

Emily smiled, though Jess sensed a quiet, troubling sadness behind the girl's gentle features.

Lisa managed a smile of her own, though it sat crooked on her ruined face, more a grimace than the desired expression of unity.

Jess worried for her.

"Lisa, I…"

"You'll need my Chevy," Lisa said, cutting her off. "It's parked around back. The keys are in the ignition. There's a first-aid kit in the glove compartment. Find my brother, Jess. Find him."

"I'll be back soon. Lisa…are you sure you're okay?"

"I think so. Yeah."

Emily reached forward and took Lisa's massive hand in her own tiny one. "You don't need to be afraid. I won't hurt you…"

Then Jess was making for the door.

31

The earth came hard and fast towards Curt.

He was back down in the dirt, breathing in the desert dust, coughing his lungs up as his fingers scraped the sand.

How many times had he fallen over now?

Five? Six? Ten?

Who gave a shit?

What mattered was the he was almost there.

He looked up, his vision blurred by pain and stinging sand. There, in the distance, stood the old house. In the darkness, he couldn't properly discern the building's shape, but there were no other houses out here. This had to be it.

Light shone from both a lower window and one higher up; two lights guiding him home, back to his Jess.

All you gotta do now is make it there.

Easier said than done.

Then pain, earth-shattering to begin with, had only grown more excruciating during his long, slow trek down the stretch of lost highway.

His right arm's condition had worsened during his journey, too. The hand was now swollen to twice its size and the bruising there had darkened to near-black. Above it, blood swelled from the makeshift bandage he'd wrapped around the agonizing wound. The bone, ever resilient, poked the denim bandage, threatening to break through. Every time he moved, bone scraped bandage and agony reigned. His left hand, shorn of two fingernails, was kid's stuff in comparison, though it still hurt like hell.

He'd picked up some new wounds along the way, too.

His knees, bare since he'd sliced up his jeans to stem the blood flowing from his arm, had been scraped bloody. Tattered skin hung from the seeping wounds, tearing further as he'd stumbled, crawled and fallen on his journey back to Jess.

And what happens when you get there? What then? Are you suddenly going to find the strength to fight Pete and defend your family? This isn't a movie, Curt. You can't just magic up the energy inspired by the power of love.

He'll kill you. And he'll have no trouble doing so.
Then he'll kill them.
Lisa, the girl.
Jess.

You're crawling back into a nightmare. Nothing waits for you there
but death and misery and a pain far worse than you're feeling now.

Fuck you, he told the voice in his head. *I'm going.*

Using his left hand, Curt pushed himself upright until he was on his knees. The lights from the house swayed in the distance, clear then fading, clear then fading.

Curt felt a fresh warmth kiss the flesh of his right arm as he moved. He looked down, almost too frightened to lay his eyes on it.

During his latest fall, the makeshift denim bandage had come loose. The huge gash beneath was spewing blood at an alarming rate. His arm was soaked. With his left hand he reached over and clasped the hanging bandage. Blood sluiced from between the folds, making his fingers slick.

Curt gritted his teeth, then he pressed down hard. He felt the bone prick the palm of his hand as he fought to tighten the bandage and stem the flow.

He had no more screams left inside him. He understood that should he pass out from the pain there'd be no waking up from it. Holding the ragged hole in one arm with the hand of the other, he used his legs to rise. Soon, he was on his feet, swaying like a tree in a sudden gust of wind, a feather on the breath of a god. He closed his eyes, allowed himself a moment to take in the cool night air.

"Move, Curt…move…" he told himself.

His body paid him no attention.

The darkness grew ever more inviting.

Then, Curt saw something.

Behind his closed eyelids, a dim light shone, moving closer, growing brighter even as darkness crept over his senses. He tried to open his eyes, but the strength had finally fled him.

A soft thrumming. The sound of a car engine. It drew closer and closer still, till it was right by his side.

He fell to his knees, finally acquiescing to the pain and the exhaustion.

That car. That engine. It sounded a lot like that old shits-mobile my sister drives. Curt grinned, as his ass fell onto the back of this feet and his torn and scraped knees were bit by stones.

"Lisa…" he muttered.

A voice he knew and loved better than the sound of his own heartbeat answered back.

"Not quite, baby. Not quite."

32

No sooner had the door swung shut and Jess had left, the girl let go of Lisa's hand. Lisa stared down at the child, her mind a confusion of fear, awe and a deep-seated maternal instinct to protect this strange, dangerous girl with her very last breath.

"Are you going to be okay, honey?" she asked Emily. She was unsure how to address the child and felt ridiculous even referring to her as such, but what else could she call her?

Emily's emerald eyes shone from behind her raven-black hair, seeming to emit an energy and strength that made Lisa's protective, nurturing instinct feel farcical.

"I'm fine," the child said. "He was never going to hurt me. He wanted to, but he mistook me for something else."

Lisa gulped hard. "What did...what did you do to him?"

Emily's eyes burned with dark intelligence. "I sent him to where he belongs."

Lisa had seen the spiders. So many of them. An impossible thing. And no less impossible than an endless army of spiders had been what happened to the ones that had remained when Pete had fled from the kitchen. They'd vaporized. She'd watched it happen. Wherever the disgusting creatures had come from, they'd found their way back.

"And...where is it he belongs?" she asked.

"In the forever place, where time is a lie."

Something deep and primal stirred in Lisa; an age old, instinctual dread that made the fear of mortality pale in comparison. It clung to her soul as the girl's luminescent eyes bored into her own.

"You *sent* him there?"

"I did."

"How?"

"I don't know."

"Can you do that to anyone?"

"I can."

"Good or bad?"

"No one is all good or all bad. Everyone is everything. Everyone is both. Everyone is everything in between."

Lisa dreaded asking her next question of the girl sat before her. The child looked tiny, frail, beautiful, but within her bristled a terrible force that was almost palpable.

"What are you?"

Emily giggled. "Jessica asked me that, too. I told her I didn't know."

"And *do* you know?"

"I lied. At least, I lied a *little*. I'm a mirror. That's how I think of myself sometimes."

"As a mirror?"

"I reflect the things I see inside of people. I bring people to the truth about themselves." The girl sat stock-still. She never blinked as she spoke. Lisa found herself immersed in the child's gaze, lost in those ever-shimmering eyes.

"I don't like lying," Emily said. "It makes me feel bad, especially when I lie to people I like. I like Jess a lot. She's kind."

Lisa allowed herself to smile.

"I know what you mean," she agreed.

"I know you do," replied Emily. "I know you hate yourself for lying as much as you do."

Lisa froze. A sinking feeling churned in her gut.

"What do you mean?" she asked.

Emily's bright green eyes brimmed with sadness. "You lie a *lot*..."

Lisa took a step back, unknowingly distancing herself from Emily. "I *never* lie to anyone. Not ever." And it was true.

Emily shook her head. Her long hair swayed like dark curtains, concealing her pale, white face. "Not to *others,* you don't. You lie to *yourself.*"

"What?"

"You lie to yourself."

"To myself?"

"All the time. You've been doing it for years."

"If...if it's true that you can see the truth of me, then you know that's not true, Emily."

"But it *is* true, Lisa. You've been lying to yourself so long, you don't even know you're doing it." Emily shuffled lightly from the kitchen chair. Her round, full-moon eyes narrowing to slits. Her face flushed, her cheeks, rose-red.

130

"I lied to *you*, too" Emily said.

Lisa felt weak at the knees. It was difficult to catch a breath. She blinked sweat from her eyes as it streamed down her forehead.

"You...you lied to me? Just now?" Lisa asked, her fear intensifying with each passing second the child's determined, pained eyes bored into her own.

Emily nodded slowly, taking another step towards the trembling, terrified Lisa. "I told you I wouldn't hurt you...that was a lie," the girl whispered.

Lisa was crying, now.

All around Lisa, the walls seemed to bend, twist and rearrange themselves. The glow dimmed from the overhead light, the faded paint on the kitchen walls peeled away, breaking apart and falling to the floor like autumn leaves, silent and almost serene. A suffocating darkness crept across the corners of the room, snuffing out the moonlight, strangling the air she breathed.

Emily's face was a portrait of regret. "Some lies are too big to ever take back..."

33

"Jess, we have to get back. Right now! It was Pete. It was all Pete. He's probably back at the farmhouse already. With Emily. With Lisa!"

Jess held his face. The drying blood that caked his visage like war paint cracked and crumbled beneath her tender touch. "Curt, I need you to calm down, okay? I need you to focus on me. Only on me. Can you do that?"

Curt forced a weary smile. It looked to Jess as he turned his head to her, like it might roll right off his neck and drop onto his lap.

He looked half-dead.

He *was* half-dead.

But only half.

Only half, Jess.

He's still here.

With you.

"Lisa's safe, Curt. So is the girl."

"But Pete..."

"You don't have to worry about Pete. Trust me."

Curt frowned, unbelieving. "Are you sure?"

"I'll tell you everything, honey, I promise, but right now, you're bleeding like a stuck pig and we have to tend to your wounds. This first, then I'll spill it. Deal?"

"Deal."

She wiped a tear from her eye with one hand as she popped the clip on the first-aid kit with the other. "You look like you've gone ten rounds with a tiger."

"I could take a tiger. It's just a big cat."

"A grizzly, then. Now shut up and let me prep this thing. We have to get you patched up right now, okay?"

"You're breaking my heart. Here I was, thinking I looked like a dashing prince, valiantly returning to save his bride."

His feeble attempt at humor stabbed her heart. After all he'd endured, there was still time for charm. He still sought fuel from making her smile.

And smile she did, for his sake.

Inside, she was screaming. He was soaked in blood.

Jess struggled to keep the panic from her voice.

"No time for vanity right now, handsome. You look like chewed hamburger. You don't smell too delicious either."

"I think I pissed myself when the van turned over."

"Lot of that going around tonight," Jess muttered.

"Huh?"

"Let's just say I'm not in any position to judge, babe. Now, just lay your head back and let me get to work."

"I'm still pretty..." he said to himself.

Jess smiled. "Yes, big guy...you're still the belle of the ball."

"Do you know what you're doing?"

"Not even close, now shut the hell up and let me work, for Christ's sake."

She reached into the small white box and searched for the bandages. There was little she could do in the moment besides stem the alarming expulsion of blood that flowed in a steady stream from his mangled arm. The wound was horrible; a bruised, bloodied mess of bone and glistening muscle. Jess swallowed hard as she surveyed the damage.

She pulled free a thick rope of bandage, speaking gently as she did so. "I need you to lift up your arm for me. And baby...it's going to sting a little."

Curt raised one blood-caked eyebrow. "You know how I hate spoilers, Jess..."

"Save the sarcasm," she said, working to unwind the thick cotton bandage. He sounded perilously close to losing consciousness, as though his words drifted from the far end of a long corridor. His face was growing more ashen by the second, taking on a sickly, death-like pallor.

There was no time for jokes.

No time at all.

"Babe...I need to do this now."

Without another word, Curt brought his good arm from its resting place on his blood-slick leg. Trembling, he slid his good hand, palm up, underneath the wound. He groaned in dull agony as he cradled the shattered arm in his palm. Jess, knowing he'd only be able to manage a few seconds of the pain to come, held the bandage close to the wound, ready to slide it beneath his arm then over it, the moment he lifted.

"This is going to suck," Curt moaned.

"You'd better believe it," she agreed. "Now lift your arm, big man. Let's get this done. You ready?"

"Not even close."

"Good...then let's make music."

"Fuck my life," he whispered, more to himself than to her.

Jess smiled gently. "I know...fuck mine, too"

Curt slowly lifted his arm. Jess had expected screams, but instead he uttered a deep, low moan that somehow sounded worse than any scream could.

"Shhhh, baby...just close your eyes. You're doing great. Hold it a little higher for me."

Curt did as she asked.

She tried to ignore the sickening way his forearm drooped lifelessly as he lifted, dangling unnaturally as gravity did its cruel work.

Jess took a quick, sharp breath.

I wish you were here, Lisa...

"I love you, husband," she whispered.

He was past responding.

Jess wrapped the bandage tight.

She'd been wrong about Curt's agonized moans.

The screams were worse.

Much worse.

34

"I didn't want to do this," Emily said, tired and sad.

Lisa heard herself whimper, her eyes darting from one terror to the next as she desperately tried to make sense of the shifting, malleable world in which she found herself. Deep inside her reeling and already fractured mind, Lisa wondered how she'd ended up here, on her knees on the kitchen floor.

Not that it *was* a kitchen anymore.

Nor a kitchen floor.

Beneath her, incredibly, there was now a carpet, soft to the touch.

"Please make it stop," she pleaded to the girl as all around the room dissolved, blurred from sight, pulsated and fluctuated. The world she inhabited becoming no more than a mirage.

The girl, though...the girl remained solid, untouched by the shifting reality, horrifyingly present. Looking at her, Lisa tried to tether herself to the sane world where walls didn't melt, where floors didn't grow carpets and where little girls played with dolls instead of souls.

Emily's eyes shone with a dark intellect, a psychic predator looming over the delicate spoils of a warring, twisting mind, sympathetic of her prey's plight, yet unwilling to subdue her terrible intent.

"I didn't do anything to you!" Lisa cried.

"I never said you did. It's what you *didn't* do..."

"I...I don't understand."

The small girl looked at her with something like pity. Her emerald eyes cut holes into Lisa's soul while the room that had been the kitchen continued to contort, shift and breathe. The darkness that had eaten the room seemed to be lifting, replaced by an icy blue light like that of the moon on a clear Mojave midnight. There was something artificial in the hollow glow. It flickered as though it fed on electricity.

Lisa shuddered as the icy radiance lit the girl in silhouette. The child, or whatever she was, stood still as stone, while reality, as Lisa had always known it, bent to the child's terrible will, wiping away the last remnants of the farmhouse, the kitchen and the sane, safe, understandable world.

"Do you ever feel alone?" the girl asked her with a disarming innocence.

Lisa, unsure of the correct response, said nothing. The eerie blue glow, that seemed to battle with the shadows, dressed the girl in a ghostly light.

"Billy felt alone, too."

Billy...

What had Billy got to do with...

"You're scared of what's coming, aren't you?" Emily asked.

Lisa thought of the spiders. Millions of hungry, crawling *things*. "Please...don't let the monsters come."

"Monsters?" Emily repeated to herself. "Oh, you mean the things that took Pete. They're not coming."

"Thank you...thank you...I..."

"But there are *other* monsters. All sorts of other monsters. There are even monsters in *our* world, Lisa," Emily said. "Monsters that wear human skin. Some of them are easy to see. They wear their corruption with pride. They delight in it. They're the ones who steal children from the schoolyard, who rape and murder in the shadows, who leave ruined bodies in muddy fields like trash.

"And then there are the *other* monsters. The ones who don't know they're monsters. The ones who should know better, who *do* know better. They cover their eyes to the evil they see. They will themselves deaf to the screams they hear, just so they can sleep easier at night, just so their lives are a little less painful. They allow the terrible things to happen. They see it, they know it, yet in their weakness, they shrivel beneath their cowardice and they do *nothing*."

The girl's eyes burned with a muted, sad fury as she spoke. Lisa, on her knees, felt tiny before the child, like a bug underfoot, set to be squashed.

"Sometimes, I think *those* monsters are even worse than the ones who revel in their foulness. The monsters like *Pete*...their souls are already forfeit. But those who allow them to wallow in their filth, when they could do something about it and *don't*...sometimes I think those are the worst kind."

Lisa was crying now. She wanted to beg, to plead, to appeal to the girl's sense of morality, but she was unable to speak. Terror climbed down her throat and nestled there, choking her, stealing her breath away.

In the dimming light, she could just about make out the details on what had once been the kitchen walls. It looked like...

The light flickered. Darkness and light. Darkness and light. Darkness and light. Faster and faster until...

All went dark.

Sobbing in terror, Lisa found herself alone, in a perfect blackness that seemed to press in on her with evil intent.

Then the room, as sudden as it had been plunged into darkness, was cast in light.

Instead of cold, crumbling yellow paint, the walls were now covered in fresh, clean wallpaper. The new decor featured stars and planets of all shapes and sizes.

There were posters on the walls, too.

One, worn at the edges, featured *Batman* swinging into action. Another displayed a fat, green character from *Ghostbusters*. On another, a green, fish-like beast held a woman in its scaly arms. She couldn't remember the creature's name, or if it even had one.

But she could remember the poster.

She could remember *that*, just fine.

Oh, god, no.

Billy had loved that poster.

It had hung on his wall till it was worn down to nothing. When she'd finally deemed it worthy of only the trash, he'd cried and cried till his eyes puffed up, red and swollen with sorrow. She swung her head around, unwilling to believe.

The kitchen table was gone. Now a bed, sized for a small boy and adorned with *Star Wars* bedsheets and pillows to match, took its place. A bedside table stood by its side, topped with a small lamp, its shade decorated by yet more bright, shining stars like those that adorned the wallpaper. Comics littered the small table, all cheerful colors and terrible detail.

It's not real. It's not real. It's not real.

"It's real," Emily stated, flatly.

"I'm not in Billy's room. I'm not here. I can't be."

Lisa bowed her head under the weight of lost memories, once more rising from the dark to take form and rip her world asunder. There was no point protesting. She was here. She was in Billy's bedroom, years in the past.

"Do you remember when he was five years old, your little boy?" Emily asked. "Do you remember how he was? It wasn't so long ago…"

Lisa nodded, tears streaming down her face.

"He was always falling down, wasn't he? He was always getting himself hurt. You'd turn your back for two minutes and he'd be cut or bruised." Emily's words dug into Lisa's soul. She sat on the soft, impossible carpet of her son's childhood bedroom and wept.

"If only you'd looked out for him. That's what you told yourself, isn't it? That if you could *only* have made more time for him. But life was busy. There were only so many hours in the day in which to do your own thing. It didn't matter how you did it…beer or drugs or both…as long as *you* were free from your own misery. That was all that mattered.

"But you knew, didn't you? You *knew* that Billy wasn't clumsy. You *knew* he wasn't falling down, or falling from his bike, or being beaten by the mean kids on your street. You *knew* what was happening to him, deep down inside you *knew*, and you did *nothing*."

Lisa's ears rang with a sound as familiar as it was unwelcome.

Her son, Billy, was crying.

His pained sobbing seemed to sound from every corner of the unreality engulfing her.

Then, as suddenly as the phantom cries were birthed, there was dead silence.

Somehow, the silence was worse.

From the center of Billy's bed, the sheets began to rise.

Just a small mound at first, then, slowly, the form beneath the sheets achieved solidity. A small hand rose from the top of the covers, lifting them downwards. She saw the messy tuft of brown hair…

Just like his father's…

Please no, this can't be…it can't be…!

Emily spoke, with a cold rage. "My father…if he ever *was* my father, used to tell me, 'evil people thrive when good people do nothing'. He said that a lot. I think in some ways he believed it. *I* believed it," Emily whispered.

"The thing is," Emily continued, "when the good people do nothing and they look after only themselves, those they should be helping get hurt…they get hurt *over* and *over* and *over* again, until a piece of them dies. Something inside them…something that should be pure and good…is lost. It can never come back. But it can *wait*, Lisa. In the dark places, it can *wait*.

"Now look what you turned a blind eye to…" the girl sneered in disgust.

On her knees, Lisa stared in horror as the bedsheets were finally pulled all the way back. There, battered and bruised from head to toe, caked in blood from a hundred cuts and lacerations, rested her son, Billy. Not as he was now, but as he'd been when he was five years old, a little small for his age, but broad shouldered, lean, strong.

Billy's head lifted from now blood-caked pillows and turned in her direction. His eyes bloodshot, peering from behind black and bruised eyelids, swollen almost shut.

He blinked red bloody tears that trickled down his cheeks.

"Why didn't you help me?" the phantom Billy whispered.

Lisa found her voice. "Oh, Billy…please, baby boy…please. I never *knew*!"

But that wasn't true, was it?

"I was lost, baby. I was *lost*. I didn't know what to do."

"He beat me, Mommy. He beat me when he was drunk."

All these years since leaving Pete, she'd grown, she'd changed, she'd found her strength. The past? She'd buried it, pushed it down deep somewhere inside. Forgotten it, moved beyond it, *denied it*. Now, all the lies she'd told herself throughout sobriety came crashing down, as, within her psyche, a tsunami of terrible truth washed away the self-deception.

"He beat me over and over and over again," Billy said. Blood spilled over his lips as he spoke, running down his tiny chin and spilling onto his chest, painting crimson the bruised flesh of his little body. He sat up straight, his soft brown hair hanging awkwardly over a dark lump, the size of a plum, that swelled from his forehead.

"Please, Emily. Please. Make it stop," Lisa begged. "I'm sorry. I'm sorry! I didn't know it was Pete doing it. I told myself it was other kids. I was depressed. I was a wreck."

It wasn't Emily who answered, but Billy.

"You'd have *known* it was Daddy, if you'd have stopped drinking and been my Mommy."

It was true.

It was all true.

She'd never been there for him. He'd endured terrible things at the hands of his father while she'd been too damn drunk to protect him, to do the one job she'd been put on this Earth to do.

A cut here, a bruise there...no big deal.

Boys would be boys.

That's what she'd told herself, during and after those terrible, wasted years. Yet somewhere, deep down inside, she'd always known. The realization crawled from its burial ground in her mind, surfacing in all its horror. Down in the darkness of her soul, she'd known. And she'd done nothing.

How many times had her son suffered since then, at his father's hands? How many times had he endured Pete's wrath, alone and afraid, because *she* was too weak to face reality head-on? Pete was a monster. She should have *seen* it. She'd gotten Curt killed, more than likely. Almost gotten Jess killed. But worse than all that, her delusion had left Billy in the cruel hands of a vicious, sick man. She looked at his bruised and bloodied body and saw every mark, every cut, every hurt his father had inflicted all at once, undeniable, a tapestry of her failure over all the long years.

Emily was right. The damage could never be undone.

"I'm so sorry," she sobbed, talking directly to him.

He was on all fours now, moving towards her, crawling across his bed. "*I'm* sorry too, Mommy."

"Billy..." Lisa wept, hopelessly.

"I'm sorry Daddy was a mean man. I'm sorry he got mad when he got drunk and I'm sorry he got a drunk a lot. I'm sorry *you* got drunk too, Mommy. I'm sorry you fell asleep so often. I'd call out for you, but you never came. You'd see the marks on me, but you'd drink, and you'd forget. You didn't help me. I was alone, Mommy. You left me all alone."

"Baby, I was weak...I...I couldn't face it. I was lost. I told myself your daddy would never hurt you like that." She lifted her head, trying to summon what spiritual strength she had left. "I can face it now, though, Billy. I can face it now."

140

The thing that was Billy smiled. It maneuvered itself till its legs were hanging over the side of the bed, then it slowly slid from the edge of the bed and stood before her.

"Yes, Mommy, you'll face it. You'll face all of it."

Lisa closed her eyes to the horror, tried to will it all away.

She felt her son's small hand brush through her hair. Her heart shattered for all the wrong she'd done.

It's not Billy. Billy's alive and well. He's far from this place and he's free of Pete. He's free of me, too. God help me, he's free of me.

But she couldn't bring herself to believe it. The part of Lisa's mind that understood this was not her son had eroded down to dust and ash. The only Billy that existed now was the beaten, bruised and accusing little five-year-old boy stood before her. His small hands left her hair, moved down her face, caressed her tear-soaked cheeks. She felt no heat in his tiny palms.

His thumbs moved to Lisa's eyes.

"Billy…"

"You can't look away anymore, Mommy. Not anymore."

Billy's thumbs pushed slowly inward.

The pressure was immediate, so was the pain. "You'll see it *all*, Mommy…forever and ever and ever…"

Lisa screamed as her son's thumbs dug into her eye sockets.

…"and ever and ever…"

She felt the delicate flesh of her eyeballs give way under the pressure. Something burst. Warm liquid splashed down her face, thick and slimy, like egg yolk.

"…and ever and ever and ever…"

Lisa screamed her agony into the endless darkness. Her son's scratching, tearing fingers probed deeper still, exploring the pulped ruins of her eyes.

"…and ever and ever…"

"Pleeeeease!" she howled, as Billy clawed the punctured, deflated orbs from their sockets.

There was a flash of intense pain. Not from her eyes, where her son had his play, but from her chest. She seized rigid, as invisible hands clutched her heart and began to squeeze till it felt it might burst.

Heart attack.

141

Thank you, God.
Thank you.

Lisa's relief at being free of the nightmare, and her gratitude to a forgiving God for freeing her, lasted right up until the moment of her death.

Then she opened her eyes anew.

35

Jess pulled up behind the old house. She killed the Chevy's engine. Around her, the sounds of the desert night seemed to swell; a coyote howled its hunger somewhere out there in the dark, a soft wind brushed the dust up around the vehicle while a silence, louder than both, breathed deep.

"Are you ready?" she asked, looking at Curt.

"You know you sound crazy, right?"

She studied his wounds. The steady flow of blood from his arm had subsided a little. His other cuts were already healing over. He'd never be the same man again, nor a mechanic, but he'd live. That was enough.

"You think so?" she asked. "What's crazy about the fact that the sweet little girl we kidnapped isn't *just* a little girl? What's crazy about the fact she can make a person's nightmares real? What's crazy about that? Sounds just as American as apple pie to me, honey."

Curt raised a weary eyebrow. "My point, exactly."

Her tone grew more serious. "I *know* it's crazy, big guy. You think I don't *know* it? What's going on in that house, with Emily…it's unbelievable, I know that. What I'm asking is, can you believe me, *besides* how crazy it is?"

Curt sighed. "You've never lied to me before."

"Not that you *know* of…"

"Not that I…*what?*"

Jess laughed. It *felt* good, necessary. "I'm just messing with you."

"What's not to believe? We kidnapped a little witch, or a demon, or…"

"Do you *believe* me," she interrupted.

He smiled his lop-sided smile. The skepticism in his eyes clearing. "I believe you."

Jess took his hand in her own. He winced but allowed her to hold it.

"So, what now?" he asked.

"I wish I knew. I guess we go in there and we all sit down and talk…you, me, Lisa…and Emily. We're off the reservation here, Curt, but we're together. All of us. Whatever else she might have done, that little girl saved Lisa's life. She saved *my* life. She's more than just a kid, but she *is* a kid, do you understand? She's good. She's kind."

"And she could kill us all, any time she chooses."

"But she won't. She won't because if she wanted to, she'd have done it long ago. There's no getting around this, baby, we brought her here to this place. We can't just bail on her. Not out here. We need to get her home. I can live with jail, Curt, if that's what fate has in store for me, but I can't live with abandoning a child. I did that once before…"

Despite the pain he must have felt, he gripped her hand reassuringly in his own. "No, Jess! You've never abandoned anyone…"

Jess remained resolute. "I can't abandon her, baby. She's my responsibility…*ours*. I owe her my life."

Curt breathed a heavy sigh of resignation. "We'll make this all right. Somehow, we will."

"Then come on. Those bandages won't hold. Not for long. You need a much better nurse than me, big guy."

"Lisa…"

"Yep…Mama Bear, herself. Come on. They're waiting for us."

36

Using his one good hand, Curt gripped the rickety wooden bannister leading up the house's outside stairs. Jess guided him as best she could. He was grateful for the comforting warmth of her arm around his waist. It didn't take the pain away, not by a long shot, but simply having her close was a blessing, just as it had always been.

He dragged his feet up the stairs, his eyes fixed on the front door. From within, the kitchen's dim light shone outwards, illuminating the porch and the old swing-chair that resided below the window. The chair swayed slowly in the cool western breeze, as though ridden by a long-traveling spirit, grateful for rest and the chance to take in the warm night.

Something was making him uncomfortable, something besides the pain from his legion of wounds, or the knowledge that there was a child with supernatural, unknowable abilities somewhere on the other side of that door. She was probably sat in the kitchen now, conversing with Lisa. Lisa had a way with kids. She loved them. Always had, even when she'd been down in the deepest depths of her alcohol-induced illness. Still, for all the love she held in her heart for the young, she carried, too, a muted sadness, always evident when she was around children. Whereas Jess had gravitated towards the little girl from the first moment, Lisa had been subdued.

He would never say anything to Lisa on the matter, but Curt had an idea why.

We all have pasts, he mused. *We all have places we've been and things we've seen. Some of those things help us shine. Some diminish us. And we don't get to choose which of them cling to our souls as we grow - the good or the bad.*

Lisa, for all her bravado and good cheer, was weighed down by a terrible guilt and though he never knew the finer details, Curt believed he knew the cause.

Had he known of her plight with alcohol or the damage it had wrought in her household – helped along in no small part by Pete, a heavy drinker himself – he'd have intervened far sooner than he had. But those had been different times and he a different man. It had been almost nine years since he'd seen his older sister when he'd showed up, unannounced, on her doorstep.

He'd missed her badly. The time had come to reconcile. He was a different man, renewed by love, able to forgive and move beyond the past. What was more, he knew that Lisa would love Jess. Billy, too.

He'd found his sister and her son living in squalor and filth.

Pete had recently left - for good, most likely - and Lisa was trapped in a depression so low he feared for her chances to pull through. Curt had made damn sure she stayed sober on that first evening they reconciled, and Lisa been sober ever since. She'd beat her addiction for her son, for her Billy, and she'd never looked back. The intervening years had washed away the awfulness of her previous life, but the scars ran deep and would always remain.

She'd been a drunk, an addict and a deadbeat mom.

She'd missed much of her son's life, having been drunk for most of his few years in the world. The things she hadn't missed, Lisa had confided to him, she'd forgotten. There was nothing there to grasp onto. Only faded snapshots, fragmented moments, confused and disjointed.

Occasionally when memories surfaced, Lisa would open up as best she could about those dark times, though he'd never urge her to probe deeper, afraid of what they both may learn. Instead, Curt had done all he could to help her move forward.

Even if it meant hiring that son of a bitch, Pete, so the bastard could pay for little Billy's upkeep.

Thinking of Pete in the light of what had transpired, Curt shivered. The man was…

…*had been*…

…a psychopath. As devious and cold-blooded as they came. He'd always known the man was no good, but in the last few hours his employee and one-time brother-in-law had proven to be something much worse.

It made Curt wonder just exactly *what* had driven his sister to the bottom of a liquor bottle. He shuddered at the thought, mentally noting that as soon as he had a chance he'd sit Lisa down and listen to her story, for better or worse.

Pete, it turned out, had been capable of anything.

Anything.

Don't think about it. There's nothing can be done about the past. Pete's dead, Lisa's alive and Billy is growing into a strong, quick-witted and kind young man. The ghosts may linger, but they can be dispelled. They will be.

His tried to clear his mind as Jess left his side and made for the door. The first-aid kit swung in her hand. She smiled at him reassuringly. "Lisa will do wonders with this. Can you stand okay?"

"Steady as a rock, honey."

"Now please, remember…she's *just* a girl. She's good. She needs our help and she saved us. She saved us all. You were great with her earlier this evening. Be great *now*."

"I'll try," he said, but he felt like he was standing on a jostling funhouse floor, his footing close to slipping at any moment. The pain was one thing. The *fear* was another.

He hadn't lied back there. He believed his wife completely.

Though he wished he didn't.

"Let's go in," she said quietly.

Jess opened the door.

She screamed.

Curt, hurtled from his fear and apprehension by desire to protect Jess, leapt forward, slamming his way into the kitchen. His broken arm screamed as it collided with the swinging door. Whatever was in there that had made Jess scream, he'd face it head on.

Curt stopped in his tracks the second he saw the horror in the kitchen. *Oh Jesus. Jesus, no.*

Lisa lay sprawled on the floor, her face frozen in a horrified scream, her hands frozen in death's snapshot, clawing at her chest.

From behind him, Jess moaned. "Oh, God."

He could barely hear her.

He stared into the black mulched pits where his sister's eyes had been…

Kind eyes. Strong.

In the abyss of her hollowed-out ocular sockets he saw madness, curled like a rattler, keen to strike out and bite into his mind as he stared helplessly into the depths.

"Lisa," he uttered, tonelessly. "Lisa…"

Jess was inside now, too. She fell to her knees before the body of Curt's older sister, the first-aid kit crashing to the floor by her side as she let it fall and reached for Lisa.

Time stood still.

He never cried. He was beyond that. All he'd been through, all he'd done to see his family survive and to give them a better life, it had come to this – his sister, dead and cold and already starting to smell – on a stranger's kitchen floor.

"It was her, wasn't it," he stated.

Jess brushed Lisa's eyelids softly, shutting them to the world, curtains closing on an empty stage. It took Jess a moment to speak. "We don't know that, Curt. Pete…Pete may still be alive."

"It was her."

"Please, Curt. There has to be a reason for all this."

"Where is she?"

As if in answer, a quiet weeping sang from the stairwell in the hall. He recognized it as the crying of a child.

Emily.

Curt spun on his heels, ignoring the dull throb of pain in his shattered arm, ignoring the deeper pain in his heart. All his attention was on that soft and quiet sobbing and the girl who sobbed.

He grabbed a table knife from the side of the sink and made for the hallway.

37

"Curt...don't!" Jess screamed, as he swept the knife from the sink and made for the hall. Curt ignored her. He paced across the floor, stepping over his sister's corpse along the way. Jess was pulling on his shirt, begging him, but she barely registered.

"I'll kill her."

"She's just a child!"

He steeled himself and moved into the hallway.

She was sat at the foot of the stairs, her head on her knees, her shoulders hitching with the force of her grief. On hearing his approach, she looked up with red, wet, agonized eyes.

"I didn't want to do it," she said.

Jess was still pulling at him. He slowed, his attention fixed on the little girl. In his hand, the knife seemed to throb with a life of its own.

"Don't do this," Jess implored from his rear. "Curt. Please. There's no coming back from this."

Though he spoke to Jess, his eyes were on the girl. "She killed her, Jess. She's a monster."

The girl's face burned red with shame.

"I'm sorry. I had to. I had to, once I saw..." Emily moaned.

"What are you!?" Curt screamed.

"I don't know," Emily answered, helplessly.

"She's a *kid,* Curt!"

"She's no damn kid."

"Look at her!"

Curt gripped the knife. He took a step closer to the girl. "Why?" he demanded through gritted teeth. "*Why* did you kill my sister!? She never hurt anyone! She was kind. She was *good*!"

Emily shook her head. "She wasn't good. She was bad! Not all the way, but she was bad! The things I saw in her heart. I couldn't allow her to be with us. It wasn't safe!"

The girl sniffed. She eyed the knife though she seemed unafraid. She wasn't crying for herself. She was crying over what she'd done, Curt understood.

"You took me from my family. I never asked to be taken, but they don't want me back. They *hate* me. I've nowhere to go. I only have you."

Her words gave Curt pause. There was truth to them. Hadn't he himself gripped the payphone every bit as tightly as he now gripped the knife, breathless with dread while it rang and rang and rang?

The girl *was* alone.

And that was on *them*.

Jess came to his side. "Give me the knife, Curt."

The girl wiped her sleeve across her face. "She allowed bad things to happen to her son."

"No…" Curt retorted, though the words felt hollow. "She would never have let Billy be hurt."

"She did! And she would have allowed it to happen again! To me! She was bad!" the girl shouted, her voice cracking with sorrow.

"Curt…the knife…" Jess implored. "You can't do this."

"Lisa…she killed Lisa."

"Look at her, Curt! She's just a scared kid! She needs us. She needs our help!"

"She's playing you, Jess, can't you *see* that!? She knows what you've been through. This…*girl*…is inside your head."

Jess held his arm tightly. "We're responsible for all of this, not her! We caused *all of it!* Pete…and Lisa…*everything*! We did this!"

"We had to!"

"To save my life, is *that* why we did it?"

"You know it is."

"And what's my life *worth*, Curt? Is it worth kidnapping? Is it worth going against everything you know to be good and decent? Is it worth selling your soul for a few more years in this cold fucking world we live in? Worth terrifying a little child? Worth *killing* one?!"

Curt felt the tension drain from him as his wife spoke. A guilt, deep and profound, rose to the surface of his psyche. Jess, damn her, was right. Whatever else the girl may be, she was a girl first. Small, frail, timid, alone.

What had they become?

Perhaps Lisa was the price he and Jess had to pay, for the choices they'd made.

He closed his eyes.

150

Lisa...

In his mind, he saw them as children.

Lisa stands in the center of their shared bedroom. In her hand, she holds a portable sound system. A 'ghetto-blaster' as they both like to call it, trying to be as hip as they could manage. Music booms from the speakers so loud he can feel it vibrate beneath his skin. She dances on the spot, spinning with her arms out and her head flung back while Led Zeppelin *howl like wild animals about a 'gallows pole', whatever that is.*

"Come on, Curt! Dance with me!" she screams, way louder than necessary.

From downstairs, their mother yells angrily. "What's all that infernal racket going on up there!? If I hav'ta come up there, I'm gonna shine both your asses good!"

They both laugh, knowing their mother as they do, knowing that 'shining their asses' is a torment they'll never suffer at her kind hands.

"Ah, the hell with it!" he hears Mom grumble, receding back into their living room.

"Dance with me," Lisa demands again.

Curt rises from the bed and stands by her side. She's taller than him by at least a head. She takes his small hands in her own and smiles down at him with gleeful abandon. "Now this here is what we call Rock 'n' Roll music, baby brother, and it's just about the greatest thing in the whole wide world!"

At fourteen years old she's a very different creature from the one she'll become. She's thinner for one thing. Thin as a pole. And achingly beautiful, too. Untouched by the ravages of a life poorly lived. Unblemished by a future that awaits her.

Tears streamed down Curt's face. Jess was saying something, but she was far away.

Before life had ran over her, in ways he both knew and did *not* know, his sister been his whole world - his hero, his protector, his friend. In the years when he'd lost her to alcohol, God only knew what she'd seen or done.

Well, not *only* God knew.

The girl knew, too.

And Lisa had died for it.

They dance in a circle, arms stretched out, Lisa grinning from ear to ear with a mischievous shine in her wide, happy eyes. "Do you like it!?" she shouts.

"I love it!" he shouts back. "I love you, as well." He has no idea why he speaks those words. They just come out. Even so, it feels right *to* say *them out loud.*

She stops dancing. She takes one of his small hands and holds it to her heart. "And I love you, squirt. Even if you are *a dweeb."*

Outraged, Curt protests. "I'm not a dweeb!"

"Are too!"

"Am not!"

Then she's laughing, full-throated and giddy. It sounds like music. It sounds like...

Screaming.

Curt's mind reeled as the memory was swept aside by the cruel present.

He saw Lisa as she was now in the room to his rear, crumpled up on the floor, her face contorted into a terrified scream that would only fade once the maggots hatched and had their fill. The dark, ragged pits where her eyes had been ripped out seemed to stare at him though the darkness of his mind, accusing him, demanding he do something. Anything.

"She's not a girl," Curt said, not to Jess, but to himself.

He gripped the knife in his good hand so tightly it hurt.

"This is for my sister, you fucking freak!"

Curt raised the knife.

38

Emily was on her feet in seconds and backing up the staircase. The tears had ceased. The regret that weighed on her young face replaced with fear, apprehension. She looked like a cornered animal.

Jess' heart lurched in her chest.

If the girl struck out at Curt...

Speaking of Curt, he was following the girl slowly. The knife held out before him, pointing directly at her.

"Curt...stop!" She grabbed his arm again. He spun on her and pushed her backwards. She stumbled backwards into a wall. Behind her a painting shook from its hook and crashed to the floor. Jess was stunned. In all their years together, he'd never laid a hand on her with anything but love.

"She has to die, Jess." He sounded like a stranger, his voice flat, emotionless, shorn of his natural warmth.

Emily backed up two more stairs, her eyes never leaving Curt as he slowly advanced.

"Leave me alone," she begged. "I didn't want to do it. I had to."

"You *killed* her!"

"She wasn't what you thought she was!" Emily's hand clutched the bannister. Her whole body shook. Her emerald eyes flashed from Curt to Jess, Curt to Jess, Curt to Jess, never resting on either.

"Jess! Make him stop!" she screamed.

"Curt! Put the knife down!" She made for him again. This time, Curt turned with the knife in his hand. "Don't come fucking near me, Jess. Please...don't come near me."

Jess froze.

Would he really hurt her? Was he that far gone? Had seeing his beloved sister, the mother of his nephew, beaten by Pete then torn asunder by Emily's will, driven him to utter madness? There was no time to ponder it. He was advancing on Emily fast.

He filled the staircase, standing between Jess and the girl. "Emily...run!"

Emily didn't run. She continued to back up slowly. Her attention now rested entirely on Curt. She moved slowly. Jess, horrified, saw the fear in the girl's eyes diminish, transform into something else - a child's natural instinct to survive, to strike out. It was close to taking her over, and when it did...

Curt would die.

And then, after that, his fate would be unspeakable.

Emily was atop the staircase now, stood on the upper landing and moving to the left, eyes set on her advancing would-be killer.

"I don't want to hurt you. Don't make me do it," she implored.

Curt moved forward, undaunted.

Did he not understand the danger he was in?

"Don't make me *hurt* you!" Emily warned, her eyes frantic.

The girl was holding back. Jess knew that at any moment she could stop him. She was trying her best. Her very best.

"Fuck you," Curt's voice trembled. He loomed over Emily, bathing her in shadow. His limp arm hung, dripping fresh blood onto the carpet, his wounds open anew during the short scuffle with Jess.

He didn't seem to notice it. Not one bit.

"I'm sorry," he said, through bitter tears.

Then he raised the knife above Emily.

Jess hurled herself at him. She clung to his back like a wild animal, clawing at his cheeks, raking his flesh, drawing fresh blood, desperately trying to weaken him, shake him from his madness. If she could get her hands on the knife. If Emily could explain her plight. If he had time to think with a sane, rational mind.

"I said *stay away from me!*" Curt roared. He twisted his hips, his good elbow smashing into Jess' face, mashing her lips. Pain throttled her senses. She tasted blood in the back of her throat. She held on tight. Curt bucked with surprising strength. In his madness, he'd found a terrible verve, fueled by rage and by grief. Jess toppled from his back, landed on her feet and steeled herself to attack again.

I won't let him kill a child. I won't.

With a guttural growl, she attacked.

Curt slugged her, hard.

She stumbled backwards, her world spinning. Stars shimmered before her eyes. Somewhere off in the distance, she heard Emily screaming. "Jess...no!"

She heard Curt, too. "Jess!"

The floor seemed to disappear from beneath her feet, then she was falling.

Jess tumbled down the stairs, screaming.

It was over in seconds.

One moment, his wife was stood there before him, and the next...

Curt never even had time to hate himself for striking her.

Jess lay at the foot of the stairs, her body crumpled in a fetal curl. She wasn't moving.

"Jesus! *Jess!*" he screamed, immediately forgetting about the girl as the red mist lifted from his fevered mind.

As quick as he could, he made for the stairs.

He was half-way down when, from behind him, Emily spoke.

"You shouldn't have done that. She was my friend."

Curt froze in place as she spoke the words.

He never turned around.

He never had the chance.

Emily's soft sobbing dragged Jess from the darkness. She came to, crumpled at the foot of the staircase, her head pounding. A sharp pain shot up and down her left leg like trapped electricity searching for a conduit. Looking down with blurred vision she saw her ankle had swollen to the size of an apple.

Sprained. Perhaps broken.

All of this she thought with perception that was adrift on a fog-ridden sea, a drunkards' assembling of a narrative.

The fog dispersed quickly though, urged on by the soft sobbing that filled her ears.

Reality hit.

It hit hard and fast.

Curt!

He hit me.

Then…

Falling.

The stairs. I must've fallen down the stairs.

She shook her head, hoping to clear it. It only made the pain intensify. Wincing, she turned her head on a neck that felt as badly sprained as her ankle, towards the staircase.

Emily…

The girl was fine. She stood atop the stairs on the landing, and when she saw Jess moving and their eyes met briefly, Jess saw terrible shock on Emily's face.

"I thought he'd killed you!" Emily cried. "I can't take it back. I don't know how!"

Jess had no strength left to answer. Nor the will.

Her attention was focused on Curt, stood between the two, perched almost exactly in the middle of the stairs, half-up, half-down. He seemed rooted to the spot. The knife he'd wielded had dropped from his limp hand and had tumbled down the steps, landing by Jess. He was staring at her, though he said nothing. His eyes brimmed with terror and pain. They seemed to bulge from their sockets. He was shaking too, almost imperceptibly. His whole body seemed charged by an intense muscular cramping that his frozen form would not allow him to express.

Despite his condition, he was horribly aware.

Jess understood that if he could, Curt would be screaming.

"Curt?" she asked, horrified. "Are you alright?"

She saw the first of them.

It wriggled from his limp half-open lips and fell to his feet where it rested like a remnant pulled from a nightmare, a tiny shard of a horror unknown.

It was a maggot.

"Oh god, Curt…"

He opened his lips wide to say something or perhaps to finally free his scream and in the black chasm of his mouth she saw with horror that Curt's teeth had eroded terribly. They jutted, black and decaying, from moldering gums. His tongue was a festering black slab of rotting meat. Maggots writhed on its putrid surface, some dug into the moist meat, feeding in a frenzy, feasting on the liquifying flesh. They piled up around the sallow skin of his rotting gums; a living, squirming nest of corpse-eaters. As Jess watched, more fell from the stinking rotten hollow of his mouth, dribbling like white drool over his cracked and putrefying lips.

"Curt!" Jess screamed, or tried to. She managed only a weak and unbelieving whine. Curt's eyes, lost and afraid, seemed to implore her, beg for an answer as his mouth worked silently, forming unspoken words around the feeding larvae that housed inside him.

This…this was *his* terror.

His personal nightmare.

The thing they'd discussed on a hundred nights and more.

Death.

Decay.

Rot.

He'd watched his mother die slowly, wasting away to nothing, and had never recovered from it. Now, it was his turn.

Jess knew there was nothing she could do to help.

It was already too late.

Somehow, in his pain and mortal terror, he reached for her. His hand shook uncontrollably, his fingers curled like those of a wizened crone's. Jess' reeled as she watched his fingernails slide from their proper place,

158

black and cracked, brittle as autumn leaves. Beneath them the rotting skin oozed thick, white pus. It dripped from his fetid fingertips like ink from a quill.

"Curt..." she moaned, paralyzed by shock and repulsion.

The skin on his forearms cracked and peeled before her eyes like sugar paper. Black blood oozed from a thousand wounds, sliding from his congealing musculature, ridden by tiny squirming forms.

She met his eyes.

He worded something more, even as his eyes seemed to bulge further from their sockets. Though his lips were now shriveled and liquifying, Jess knew what he wanted to say. She knew. She saw it in his hideously bulbous eyes.

"I love you too," she moaned in despair.

Then Curt's eyes slowly slid from their sockets, pushed out from within. They swung on blackened stocks upon his sunken, dead cheeks, as a sickening swell of bloated maggots pushed their way out through the sockets, escaping from his decaying cranium into the light of the world.

Jess screamed.

Curt collapsed in a heap.

The maggots feasted.

Soon there was only a putrefying soup, peppered with bone, and a million maggots writhing in exquisite, ravenous delight.

41

Her senses swamped by horror and heartbreak, Jess watched the maggots feed. She wanted to meet the girl's eyes, but found she couldn't even glance in the child's direction.

Better to witness the rapid corrosion of her beloved than meet the child's gaze.

She could sense her though, standing there, perched on the stairs and watching the scene unfold.

Curt...

He was gone.

They said that when a person faced death, all their whole life would flash before their eyes, a stop-motion grindhouse epic documenting all the pain, all the love, all the struggles and all the joy.

Jess had watched Curt's eyes. She'd seen nothing there besides torment and pain. He'd left this world via a shrieking plunge into the abyss.

"Bring him back," she demanded, her eyes still fixed upon the bubbling muck splashed out on the stairs before her.

Stupid. Ridiculous. There was no coming back.

Yet she demanded it all the same.

"Emily..." she spoke through gritted teeth and quivering lips. "Bring him back."

She sounded small, weak, ashamed. Even frightened. "I can't!" she said.

Of course she couldn't.

Jess squeezed her eyes shut and, within, Curt danced in the throbbing half-light of her mind's eye. Smiling, laughing...

Then rotting.

Her eyes snapped open, flitting from the rotten soup to the staircase. She couldn't bear to meet the girl's eyes, though she stared at her small feet. It was all she could manage.

"I didn't want to do it," Emily said, sniffing. "I liked him. But he was going to kill me."

Jess's words sounded flat and terrible in her own head. "That's the second time you've said as much, Emily. The second time."

"He wanted me dead."

"He was afraid of you. He was right to be."

"I wouldn't have hurt him."

Finally, Jess and the girl connected, eye to eye.

"He was *good*."

"I know he was."

"He was my *husband*," Jess sobbed, the full weight of her loss seeping into her pores like rot into a scabrous wound. "He was the father of my child. And you…you killed him."

"You *saw*!" the girl implored.

"I did. It's true. I saw."

"He blamed me for his sister!"

"Shouldn't he have?"

"No! I did what I had to. She was bad, Jessica. She was bad, deep down where no one knew it. She wasn't like him, or like you."

"Who gave you the power to judge over who is and isn't worthy of this life, Emily? Can you tell me that?" Jess held the child's eyes, firm, demanding an answer.

Emily, chin pressed to her chest, shook her head. Her bottom lip protruded a little, quivering. She looked close to not only crying but to bubbling, just like any other sad and scared little girl would do.

"I wanted us to be safe. To be happy… That's all I wanted."

Jess laughed. It sounded cold and harsh and so unlike herself that she wondered momentarily if someone had entered the room without her knowledge.

No one there.

Just the girl. And her. And what was left of her husband, congealing on the staircase.

"What do you think this *is*, Emily?"

"I don't understand."

"You and I…what do you think we are?"

Emily's sadness dripped from her voice like tears. "We're together. You said you'd never let anyone hurt me. You said that."

Jess took a deep, ragged breath. "I did. I said that." Jess paused, taking in the child, lost and afraid, deadly, yet as frightened as any child in dismay.

"And I meant it, Emily. I *still* mean it. God help me, I still mean it."

161

Emily's eyes filled with light. She lifted her small head and parted her hair, staring at Jess with a child's hope, perfect and heartbreaking.
Slowly, the girl moved down the stairs, avoiding Curt's remains. She knelt by Jess' side, laying her small hand in Jess' own. She felt then girl's warmth surge through her.

"I love you," Emily whispered. "You're the only person in the world I've ever really loved. Mom and Dad...they were never my parents. They looked after me, but they were never mine. I was *glad* when you took me. I was *glad* when they didn't answer the phone, and I'm *glad* I'm with you now."

"He was a good man," Jess repeated, though to herself or Emily, she didn't know.

Who the hell was she trying to convince?

Jess thought back over all that had happened.

The kidnapping of a child, bringing her to the old house, subjecting her to a man like Pete.

They should have *known* what he was.

Curt, knife in his hand, set to sink the blade into the flesh of a small child.

It was true. He would have killed Emily.

Another second and he would have killed an eight-year-old child.

And Lisa? The girl seemed genuinely distraught over the situation, but she'd hinted at something deep and dark and terrible in the big woman's past that had scraped her soul raw.

Was the girl lying?

No. There was no lie in the child. Jess was as sure of that as she was of the sun rising each day. Whatever atrocity resided in Lisa's heart, it had been severe and it had been terribly real.

"I need to tell you something, Emily."

"Please."

Jess clutched Emily's hand tight in her own, amazed by the swell of love she still felt for the girl despite all that had transpired.

"Five years ago, I..." Jess swallowed hard, determined to get through it, to share her story with Emily, to help her understand. She took a deep breath and began again.

"Five years ago, I gave birth to my daughter...my little Petra. Only...it wasn't really my daughter that I gave birth to. For Petra, there was no birth. Not really. The precious little life who'd been growing inside me for nine months was already gone. She never survived the procedure. What I gave birth to was no more than an empty shell, Emily. A beautiful, perfect, tiny shell that housed nothing inside. She died during the moment of her birth, Emily, and I died right there with her, right there on the operating table. When I met you...when we *took* you...I felt myself drawn to you. Your kindness, your heart, your spirit. I thought to myself that if my little girl had lived...if she'd made it into the world and had the chance to grow and learn and find her feet...I'd want her to have been just like you.

"That's how I felt, Emily. I didn't really spend any time around children, even on the occasions when I had the chance...birthday parties, family events, those sorts of things. I never showed. I couldn't bear to see another's child in their arms. Smiling, playing, giggling, holding onto their mommy with a love my poor sweet baby girl would never know."

Jess paused. "Do you already *know* all this, Emily?"

Emily squeezed her hand, "Does it matter? Tell me."

Jess nodded. "After she was...born...my life went to pieces. *I* went to pieces. I began drinking, like the way Pete did."

"Drinking is bad."

"Yes, in some ways it is, when it's done too often. It's a drug, Emily. Do you know what drugs are?"

"Not really. I see stuff in movies, so I know they're bad, too."

"Anyway, the alcohol wasn't *nearly* a strong enough drug to smother the pain I was feeling."

"What happened?"

"I did something I swore I'd never do. Something I'd always found disgusting, pathetic, and weak...I began smoking something called Heroin."

"I know what *that* is. That's a *really* bad drug, isn't it? All the gangsters have shoot-outs over it."

"It's a *very* bad drug, yes. I smoked it for a while. And it helped, for a while. But soon even that wasn't enough to wash away the misery. Curt tried to make me stop and to make me look for other ways to fix my broken heart, but there was no stopping it. I moved onto injecting it."

"Why did you do that, if you knew it was bad?"

163

"I'd wake up in hell every morning, lost in thoughts of my poor dead baby, robbed of her very first breath, and I'd cry. I'd cry, and I'd sink someplace deep down inside of my soul that I never knew existed. The pain I felt, Emily…it was unbearable. I knew that I wasn't strong enough to take it."

"The bad drug made it go away?"

Jess smiled bitterly, taken aback by the girl's simplistic appraisal of the hell she'd suffered. "I'd see my daughter's cold, still body everywhere I went, even behind my eyelids when I tried to shut her memory out. She was always there, always still, always *dead*. Until I took the drug, and then…"

"Then?"

"Everything would fade away. *She* would fade away. The world became pure light, my body *sang*, my pain would disappear. I felt peace."

"It doesn't sound so bad."

"It was, and it wasn't. It released me from my pain, but it killed my soul, too, Emily." She faced the girl. "And really, it killed my body, as well. All it took was one time, sharing the wrong needle. Have you heard of HIV and AIDS?"

Emily nodded.

"There's a bad kind, and a *very* bad kind…I have the very bad kind. And it stops me from having any more children, Emily. God help me, it stops me from taking the risk. If my baby was born with the disease…"

"I'm sorry," Emily replied.

"Don't you know all this?"

"I see fear. I see sin. I don't see everything."

"Perhaps that's a blessing."

"But what you did wasn't sinful. You're not a bad person."

"I'm dying, Emily. Without the proper treatment, I'm finished. Curt and I…" She paused, choking on the sound of his name. "Curt and I…we tried everything. We worked hard, and we did everything we could."

"Why couldn't you get help? Couldn't you have gone to a doctor or a hospital?"

"Those things cost money, Emily. A lot of money. We just couldn't afford the help I need. All I had…*have*…to look forward to, is a slow and painful death. I'm so scared, Emily. So scared."

"That's why you took me."

It wasn't a question. Emily had tears in her eyes. Jess, despite the things the girl had done, wanted to hold her, comfort her, tell her everything would be okay.

But that was a lie.

The girl was alone, and in huge part it was Jess' fault. By bringing her out here, she'd forced the girl to face uncomfortable things, heart-breaking things, about her own family and how they felt about their child.

And now, what was Jess to do?

Leave the girl alone out here in this accursed house, with no way to reach the outside world, alone and afraid, with little food and even less water?

No…she couldn't do that.

The girl had done terrible things, violent things…things Jess could scarcely comprehend. She had power the likes of which could reshape the world, and she'd used those powers in horrible, despicable ways, but she'd been scared. Scared out of her mind. She'd watched Pete, a stranger, almost kill both herself and Lisa, and in her mind Lisa had been a significant threat. She'd been panicked, terrified, ashamed and alone by the time Curt had went at her with the knife.

Emily had been frantic. She must have been beside herself with fear. Were her actions understandable? Were they perhaps even justifiable?

They were hard questions, with no real answers.

One thing, Jess understood, was certain.

You can't walk away from this. You can't leave her out here in this god-forsaken desert, all alone. Curt's gone. Lisa's gone. They're all gone. It's all on you and you know it. This whole thing.

All on you.

"We can get the money."

"What?" she asked the girl, her reverie broken.

"For you. For your illness. We can get the money. There are ways we can get it, and then you can get help and we can be together."

"It's too late for me, Emily. I don't deserve the help anymore. Not after all…this. Maybe I never did."

"That's not true."

"It's true."

"I *need* you, Jess." Emily was openly weeping. Her small hands clenched and unclenched the fabric of Jess' shirt as her anxious eyes implored. "I have no one."

"Don't say that."

"Jess?"

"Yes?"

"I want *you* to be my Mommy from now on. And I'll be a good girl. I won't hurt anyone. I'll be the best daughter you could hope for. I promise."

Hope poured from the child's words.

Terrible, desperate, beautiful hope.

Jess closed her eyes tight, and there in the dark, waiting as she always waited, was the memory of her poor dead Petra.

Jess, her heart hollowed out, her eyes afire with disbelief, stares down at the tiny dead thing in her arms. Her daughter, her only child, lost to her, cradled in her arms as though sleeping. She tenderly caresses her cheek. She's already growing cold to the touch. Jess opens her mouth and begins to scream. She screams until her throat tears and her heart reverberates, and a blackness, deeper and darker than any night she's ever known, envelops her soul. She screams until something snaps in her mind. She can hear it ringing in her ears.

The sharp pinprick of the needle puncturing her skin, as the doctor injects her with a sedative, comes as a welcome release. She fades, and as she does, she hopes and prays that she'll never wake back up.

Jess opened her arms. "Come here."

Emily, releasing Jess' shirt from her tight grip, opened her arms in return, and fell into Jess' warm embrace.

To Jess, it felt like belonging.

"I love you, Jessica," the girl whispered in her ear. Jess felt Emily's breath tickle her. She could smell the girl's hair, a pleasant blend of strawberry and sweat. For just a second, she allowed herself to believe…to believe that the girl in her arms was her long-dead daughter.

"I love you too, Emily. And I'm so sorry."

Jess plunged the knife into little Emily's stomach, and as the girl's warm blood began to flow down her hand, seeping between her shivering fingers, she howled her despair, just as she had when she'd held her stillborn child, and felt the world spin out of orbit, into dark, empty space.

42

Jess, drenched in sweat from exertion, laid the girl's body on the bed. Comics, paperbacks and soft plushies surrounded the child as her little form sank into the bedsheets. She looked peaceful. The slightest of smiles rested on her face.

Jess held her cooling hand in her own, squeezing it gently, missing the warmth, second by second, as it drained from the girl's body.

The night was silent now. All the madness, all the confusion, the fear, the violence…it all seemed a million miles away. A distant fever dream, a storm that passed out of perception and on into memory.

She held the knife in her hand. Emily's blood stained the blade, but Jess had no problem with that. Soon, she'd run the serrated blade across her own neck, and her blood would mix with Emily's. Together, they'd lay there in the room, side by side, and sleep, while the sun rose on a brand-new day.

She wasn't afraid anymore. Not of dying, not of pain, not of heartbreak. Soon, she'd be free of all of it. One quick motion, left to right, across her throat, and then she could lay back beside the beautiful little girl's body, and kiss the lips of forever.

She'd never hurt anyone before. Certainly, she'd never stabbed anyone. She shuddered as she relived the moment. The way Emily's skin pressed down under the blades pressure, then the tip sinking in, deeper and deeper, till Emily's final pained breath had fully expelled, one long sigh, too old and tired and wise to pass from such delicate lips. It had broken Jess' heart to do it, but killing the girl had been a mercy. She knew that. The girl's powers were too dangerous, too diabolical to be allowed to develop and evolve further. The child would have been hunted as a monster. The family she'd desired, always out of reach. Alone in an uncaring, suspicious world. And the girl's intent to help Jess get well? Jess knew that Emily's plan to get the money would have led to more bloodshed. Probably that of the girl's parents.

There'd been enough death.

And death, she knew, was far from the worst of it.

What happened to those who fell victim to Emily's power *after* death, that was what truly horrified. Jess believed the girl implicitly when she'd talked of the dead finding their souls trapped in that other place. The bad place. She'd seen a tiny glimpse of it herself. Emily was sending souls to an early damnation. One which time, fate and a lifetime's redemption may have spared the victims from suffering.

Jess tried not to think of Curt or where he was and would remain. He'd been right to try to rid the world of the child, however unthinkable. He'd been right.

It was better this way, with Emily gone and the world free of whatever she was set to become as she grew into adulthood.

Better.

Licking a tear from her parched, busted lip, Jess sat on the bed, beside the girl.

She raised the knife to her throat.

It felt cold there, against her skin. She swallowed hard and felt the knife's edge rise and fall upon her flesh. She wondered if it would hurt and found she didn't really care. It would be quick. It would be final. She gulped hard, feeling the blade catch upon skin.

Silently, Jess began to countdown from three.

Three...

She closed her eyes.

Two...

She gripped the knife's handle tight.

One...

From behind her, a small, unmistakable voice.

Though weak and distant, the venom in Emily's words froze Jess' heart.

"I thought you were *good*, Jessica. But you're *bad*," Emily snarled, all sulk and rage.

Oh Jesus, no!

The knife dropped from her hands as fright seized her.

No!

She'd been sure the girl was gone. Dead. She was *sure* of it. She'd checked for a pulse. She'd watched Emily's pupils dilate as the life fled her tiny body and her vision spun towards eternity. She'd felt the girl's flesh go cold.

She couldn't be alive!

Jess had no time to speak, no time to contemplate her mistake.

From under the bed came a high-pitched cry, terrible and pleading, pathetic, traumatized.

The cries of an infant.

Jess would recognize the owner of those cries anywhere, though a single sound had never passed those cold dead lips.

It was her baby. Her long-dead daughter.

Gripped in the maws of shrieking terror, Jess lunged forward for the knife. It lay before her on the carpet. If she could get it in time! If she could just end it...slice her own throat open and escape the child's wrath.

There was no outrunning eternity.

Jess gripped the knife. Her dead child's cold, tiny hand gripped her wrist, horrifyingly strong.

The infantile weeping changed.

It grew cold.

Devoid of inflection.

Dead.

Maleficent.

Infinitely evil.

The whole horror lasted no more than two seconds, three at most.

The tiny hand twisted. Jess heard the crackling of bone as her wrist bent backwards. Blood spewed from the mangled veins as her skin ripped and her bones ground together, then snapped. Instinctually moving into the path of least resistance, Jess fell to her knees on the carpet. The baby's hand receded into the darkness beneath the bed.

The knife!

Still time.

Laughter poured from the shadows.

This time, the horror beneath the bed used both hands.

It grabbed Jess by her ankles, and pulled.

Jess was dragged, screaming and wailing, into the darkness, where a tiny form, abominable and cruel, waited for her, its un-beating heart filled with cold, cold love.

43

She awoke on her back under the harsh, cold glare of a blinding light. Electricity hummed like a summer's honeybee while her vision swung like a pendulum from clarity to distortion.

Where was she?

She remembered screaming.

She remembered horror, and bloodshed, and terror, black as death's suffocating shadow.

And she remembered one little girl with eyes that shone green like sunlight through summer leaves, and a smile that brimmed with intellect and lit her eyes with cheer.

Squinting her eyes against the cold light that shone above her, Jess began to scrutinize her surroundings.

Besides the overhead light, the rest of the room was eaten up by a thick blackness, and though she couldn't *see* anything beyond the light's radiance, she sensed things moving amidst the gloom beyond, like hungry wolves regarding a campfire, camouflaged by the night. Looking down at her body, Jess saw she was lain on some sort of hospital bed. Her legs were parted, her knees brought up towards her waist, the legs held in place by thick white harnesses.

She realized with a dawning horror that her arms, too, were bound and held tightly in place. They lay flat, palms down on the cold white, sweat-sodden sheet.

In her mind she saw a knife.

She'd been going to use it, hadn't she...the knife?

On who?

On herself.

Why?

The girl.

Something to do with the girl...

In the splinter of a moment, it all hit.

The girl. Her dark gift. Her power over...

Death.

No!

Please Jesus. Please God. If anyone is out there, please take me home, away from here, I beg you.

Her senses were returning now, and in the hollow glow of the strange dark place in which she found herself, she began to comprehend.

She was on an operating table.

From somewhere before her, where the unseen shadows moved within shadows, Jess heard a soft cry. She peered between her legs into the darkness as fear rose in her soul like a black wraith.

Something was coming.

It moved slow, and its low position on the floor made it impossible to see its approach.

But she could hear it.

Not only its soft, lilting cries, but the shuffling of tiny hands and knees on a cold, hospital floor.

Please, Jesus, take me away from this place. Please. I'm sorry. I'm sorry for everything. Pleeeeease!

The shadows around the operating table grew restless, excitable. Through the murk, with eyes adjusting, Jess could make out the frocks and masks of surgeons, their garments grey and filthy, caked in black blood, stained with infection.

"Help meeee!" she wailed into the void that surrounded her, pungent with death.

One of the infernal doctors stepped from the shadows. He, if it was a man, loomed tall over her. Behind the filthy mask, she could see no eyes. The smell of feces poured from the surgeon in stomach-churning waves. It moved around the table till it was stood before her bare, and parted, legs.

Then, silently, it bent towards the floor.

When the hellish surgeon stood up straight again, Jess' knew her prayers were all in vain.

Held in its bloodied surgical gloves was her daughter. Stillborn, dead yet alive, already rotting, her skin a thin grey covering, stretched over tiny, brittle bones. The baby's eyes were gone. In their place...black pits, deep as the deepest well, and in them Jess saw forever.

The surgeon laid the dead child on the table between Jess' sweating, trembling, wide-open legs, and the dead child began to crawl.

It crawled towards the soft, warm center between Jess' legs, then disappeared from sight.

Jess felt small hands probe the tender, sensitive lips of her vagina, prying them open, then delving deeper, growing more frantic as it explored the soft meat inside the welcoming orifice.

Then came the agony, the blood, the ripping and the tearing.

Jess begged for death, while her dead daughter slowly worked her way back inside, first one arm, then the other, then her tiny head, lubricated by the blood pouring from Jess' torn and mangled vagina. Jess stared in horror as her stomach distended, growing larger and more pregnant by the second as the baby clawed its way back inside her body, returning to the safe, warm place from which it had once entered the world of the living. It settled, content, inside its rightful home. Back within the tomb of its mother's worthless womb.

Jess shrieked one last prayer for salvation.

The black void swallowed her prayer whole.

EPILOGUE

Emily sat on the porch chair, rocking slowly as she watched the rising sun. It peeked over the distant mountain range, heralding a day that promised clear blue skies, far as the eye could see. It was beautiful here, and despite all that had happened she felt a quiet peace swell within her. In the distance a titmouse sang a song for the Mojave morning. Emily closed her eyes, listening intently to the lonesome melody.

Wincing, she idly fingered the wound in her belly where Jess had slid the knife into her. It hurt a lot, but the wound had almost stopped bleeding now that she'd stuffed cotton into the gash and bandaged the wound.

She'd found the first-aid kit as though by luck, tripping over it as she'd stumbled from her supposed death-bed and into the kitchen, making for the door. Emily had acted as her instincts demanded. She seen enough movies to understand the basics. She almost giggled, realizing that it was her parent's neglect that had forced her to retreat into the world of movies, and it was the movies that may well have saved her life.

Everything came around in the end.

The white bandage was stained dark red and the red was slowly spreading, but if she got help...

She was feeling almost strong enough to move.

One hour had passed since Jess had betrayed her. One long hour, in which she'd sat on the porch chair, and cried all the bitter tears she had left to cry. She'd never once thought to look under the bed where Jess' remains rested. She had no desire to see the state of the kind woman's corpse. It would only inspire sorrow. Despite what Jess had done, Emily missed her. She missed her smile. She missed her touch. She missed the way Jess would comfort her, even knowing what she knew of Emily's gift.

And what *was* her gift? She had no idea. It seemed no one did. Her mother and father, though she rued to call them such, were every bit as fearful as Jess and her companions had been.

Every bit as suspicious.

174

Every bit as disappointing.

She vowed that she'd never go back there to that cold, loveless home, decorated in the finest furnishings, admired by all who visited, yet in truth as cold and desolate as a tomb.

No, she'd leave them to their riches and their fear. She felt no bitterness towards them, no pain. The time for that had long since passed.

She mourned Jess, though.

Just the thought of the kind woman made her want to cry her heart out anew.

She focused on the shifting sands beyond the porch, hoping to dispel the image of Jess that haunted her so. In the last twenty-four hours, she'd learned that to trust implicitly, even if the person seemed wonderful, was never going to be an option. Her guard, from this day on, would have to remain up.

But it wasn't all bad.

In the time she'd spent in the beautiful old house she'd learned that *she* herself was capable of something that she'd never imagined...

She was capable of *hope*.

Jessica had proven to be a failure as a mommy, it was true, but until their meeting, Emily had simply accepted her lot in life – to live a life bereft of love. She'd acquiesced to existing in a world of comic books and video games, movies and flights of fancy within her own mind, prepared only to ever view the world through a prism of her own imagination. With Jess, she'd found someone special. Someone that – had events transpired differently, she had no doubt - would have loved her with as much devotion as she would have loved her own child.

The circumstances had been wrong, that was all. Jess had suffered too many losses in too short a time. It had driven her to madness.

She wiped away her tears and closed her eyes.

A cool breeze picked up, whipping the Junipers into a gentle dance. They swayed on the morning air, and on hearing their leaves rustle in the wind, Emily was soothed. Even the deep pain in her belly seemed far off.

She wondered where she'd go from here. She was alone, she was hungry, she was tired, and she was hurt, but her spirits soared. It was a big world out there with a whole lot of people in it – some kind, some not so kind – and if her time with Jess had taught her anything, it was that she yearned to be loved, to find her proper place in the world, with a mom and a dad and maybe a little puppy she could call her own.

Whatever else was to become of her, as her powers grew and her understanding of herself deepened, for now she was a kid, and a kid needed a family.

Next time, she'd make sure she chose more wisely. And her gift? She'd keep it hidden away.

The morning was growing hotter now, and sad though it made her, Emily knew it was time to go. No one was coming down this old lonely road any time soon. If she wanted to find help she'd need to do the looking for herself.

She rose from the old swing-chair and made for the stairs. She'd lost her footwear during the kidnapping, besides her socks, and her kidnappers hadn't supplied her with shoes or sneakers, so she'd have to walk carefully.

Every few steps she'd turn and look at the house, wishing things had been different, allowing the pain to enforce her will, strengthen her determination.

After thirty minutes or so, the house faded from sight. No more than a memory, both bitter and sweet.

It took an hour to walk from the old house to the place where the dirt road joined the main highway. By the time she'd arrived, the bandage around her wound was sodden, and her feet bled from a hundred cuts. She paid none of the wounds any mind.

They'd heal just fine.

She had faith in her destiny.

Exhausted, she hoisted herself up onto an old wooden post, glad to have her raw, torn-up feet off the ground, happy to rest her little legs after walking so far. She watched the dust dance on the hot concrete of the highway. It made her think of old cowboy movies she'd watch alone in her room back home. The sort of movies where the heroes were always pure, and the women always proud. Where they looked after their children and sometimes died to protect them.

Emily smiled at the thought.

Out here where the dust and sand seemed endless, dreaming came easy.

She'd sit, and she'd wait, and eventually...

Eventually someone would come her way.

Someone *good*.

Hours passed. One then another, then another, until the burning sun hung high in the sky. And Emily, her faith in her future made whole, waited patiently. She grew weaker as the sun crossed the sky, but she was never afraid. Help would come.

Her patience, and her faith, paid off.

When, after so long and wearisome a wait, she heard the distant rumbling of a car engine and turned to see the tiny metal object glinting in the sun, shimmering like a mirage, Emily laughed aloud. It hurt, but it was worth it.

Perhaps the car was owned by a family, driven by a loving father. Perhaps they were on their way to a holiday destination. Perhaps they were young lovers, keen to build a home, build a family...

The possibilities seemed as endless as the Mojave itself.

She'd behave as best she could. She'd do as she was asked. She'd keep her secret all to herself, and if they resisted or turned out to be bad people...

Emily had a solution for that, too.

Hopping from the worn wooden fence-post, she limped to the side of the road. She glanced back only once, not seeing it, but knowing the house was out there. The house where she'd learned to dream of a better life. The house that now stood in silence. The house that was no longer a house, but a tomb sheltering the body of her poor, lost friend.

"Bye, bye Jess," she whispered.

On the warm desert wind, she imagined she heard screaming.

Emily turned to the highway.

And raised her thumb.

THE END

Afterword

Thanks for sticking around. I hope you enjoyed the story.

I know I had a lot of fun during my time spent with sweet little Emily, getting to know her, suffering with her, fearing her, and in the end, hoping for a better life for this strange, wise girl. I came to see her as both my protagonist *and* antagonist, and I wanted to allow you guys to view her in whatever manner suits your perception.

Whether villain or foe in your mind, I hope you found Emily to be a fun and fascinating character. I often feel that when too much is given away by the author, a story can lose the ferocity of its *bite*, or at least its sense of mystery, of the uncanny. For me, she's a mirror in many ways. She reflects many of my own fears growing up, and many of my hopes, too. I like her a lot, and would love to spend more time with her. Whether I do or not, only time will tell. I can envision all sorts of fates for her, but a part of me just wants to leave her as is - by the roadside with her thumb held high, eight-years old, and with her future and her purpose left as an open book.

Maybe it's best that way. Not everything need be explained, and not all stories need to be told.

We'll see.

For now, I got what I need from Emily and she took what she needed from me. What she'll take from the poor people in that car, who knows.

I dread to think...

Let's hope they're good people. Good enough to stay on her sweet side.

Thanks for reading, guys.

I hope to see you for the next one.

Your pal,
Kyle

Other works by the author:

Anthologies
Consumed Volume 1
Consumed Volume 2

Novels
Devil's Day
Aftertaste
Where the Dead Ones Play
The Club

Razorblade Candies
(Novellas)
Love Lies Dead
VHS
The Wild
Tradition

Contact Kyle at –
authorkylemscott@outlook.com

Made in United States
Troutdale, OR
09/13/2024

22796566R00106